VEE R. PAXTON

The Ring of Souls

Voices of Vernaria Book One

First published by WOOW Books 2021

Copyright © 2021 by Vee R. Paxton

All rights reserved. No part of this publication may be reproduced, stored or transmitted in any form or by any means, electronic, mechanical, photocopying, recording, scanning, or otherwise without written permission from the publisher. It is illegal to copy this book, post it to a website, or distribute it by any other means without permission.

This novel is entirely a work of fiction. The names, characters and incidents portrayed in it are the work of the author's imagination. Any resemblance to actual persons, living or dead, events or localities is entirely coincidental.

Vee R. Paxton asserts the moral right to be identified as the author of this work.

Vee R. Paxton has no responsibility for the persistence or accuracy of URLs for external or third-party Internet Websites referred to in this publication and does not guarantee that any content on such Websites is, or will remain, accurate or appropriate.

Designations used by companies to distinguish their products are often claimed as trademarks. All brand names and product names used in this book and on its cover are trade names, service marks, trademarks and registered trademarks of their respective owners. The publishers and the book are not associated with any product or vendor mentioned in this book. None of the companies referenced within the book have endorsed the book.

First edition

ISBN: 9798531612779

Editing by Peter Lancett
Cover art by JS Designs

This book was professionally typeset on Reedsy.
Find out more at reedsy.com

For my mother and in memory of my father.

Contents

Foreword	iii
Acknowledgement	iv
Prologue: Five Years Ago	1
A Mysterious Invitation	3
The Proposal	16
An Unexpected Discovery	28
The Magic Man	39
Second Thoughts	46
Enchantment	57
Danger Abroad	66
The Warrior	74
The White Lady	80
Questions	86
The Escort	91
Sisterhood	102
A Family Affair	109
Foreign Rituals	114
Family News	120
A Royal Visit	125
Experimentation	132
A Message from Beyond	142
Strange Dreams	154
The Whirling Warrior	160
A Quiet Evening	168
The Room	172

Keeping it Together	180
The Gift	184
Healing Magic	188
Something is Coming	198
Souvenirs	202
Truths	205
Ruins	215
Rude Awakening	218
The Missing Bride	222
About the Author	226

Foreword

The White Rose
"The red rose whispers of passion,
And the white rose breathes of love;
O, the red rose is a falcon,
And the white rose is a dove.
But I send you a cream-white rosebud
With a flush on its petal tips;
For the love that is purest and sweetest
Has a kiss of desire on the lips."
-John Boyle O'Reilly - 1844-1890

Acknowledgement

I'm honored to have so many amazing souls to thank.

To Neil Gaiman, for inspiring the completion of this novel. In your MasterClass, you said to finish things. I did, and I will continue to do so.

To Peter Lancett, for getting out your amazing polishing cloth and offering your wisdom as my editor. You went so far above and beyond what was asked of you. I'm a better writer for listening to you.

To my mother, Barbara, for always being there for me and believing in me. You've encouraged me to do this for years. Thanks for believing in me.

To HC, I couldn't have created this without your inspiration.

To my friend Erica Jade who taught me to believe in myself, my talents and embrace a life I love.

To Michael for enduring all of my ups and downs on this journey and being there for me through it all.

To Natalie, Beth, Flor, Laura, Diane, Cristina, and all my other supporters, readers. listeners and friends who've been guiding and encouraging me. You all know who you are and how much I love you. .

Last but not least to my cat, Ramses, for sitting on my computer and making sure I took breaks.

Prologue: Five Years Ago

Maeve looked out at the night sky. The blackness told her it was time, no moon tonight. She made her way down the stone stairs at the back of the manor, her special items in the simple sack she carried. As she passed the opening to the sea, she paused to look again. The smooth sounds of the waves hitting the beach signaled a calm sea. She smelled the salt in the air, enjoying the breeze on her face. After a few breaths, she ran her fingers through her thick red hair as a comfort to steady her resolve. She continued down the path into the deepest part of the manor, to the very source of her magic. Tonight she would increase that power tenfold. At her destination, she looked across the large stone room. There it was, the source of her family's power, the gate that held the spirits of her ancestors. She stood in front of it as she had done hundreds of times before.

At the center of the large stone ring, there were varying shades of blue swirling around. The voices of her ancestors whispered to her, trapped in this cage to aid in her magic.

"I am here, my love, awaiting your instructions," she announced.

Inside the ring, the images began to move more quickly. They swirled in a dance of light and color. The entities near the front retreated as if terrified of what was moving forward. A large dark shape filled the circle.

"My most prized student." The voice from behind the gate was deep and clear. "Have you made all of the arrangements? Have you brought me the items as instructed?"

"Of course. I have also set things in play as instructed. Your faery half-breed prize will be among us in due time. My son will see to that."

"Beautiful Maeve. In all the centuries I have been trapped here, few have dared to call me, but you have been my most loyal, most prized student. Are you ready to join with me? Are you ready to combine our powers?"

Maeve steadied herself. She'd allowed brief possessions from ancestral spirits in the past, but this was different. Maximilien was one of the most ancient of her ancestors, his power in life had been one of the most formidable in her lineage.

"Yes, darling. I am ready." Maeve took in a deep breath and began her ritual. As she chanted, she heard cries among the ghosts. Screeches echoed in the chamber as Maximilien performed his own ghostly ritual from behind the veil of death. A crimson light began to form at the front of the gate. Orbs of orange, red and yellow began emanating from Maeve. The lights inside and outside the circle reached for each other as she chanted louder. With a loud clap, the lights merged and immediately poured into Maeve. The dark, shadowy form of Maximilien was no longer visible behind the gate. Maeve was bathed in the warm fiery light. She smiled. She could feel him inside her head. They were together at last. From behind the gate, the voices cried.

"What have you done?"

A Mysterious Invitation

It felt odd to know that as of tomorrow, I'd be homeless. I'd traveled plenty in the past three years, but this home spot had always been here. Tomorrow I was giving it up. Staying here without Gran was too heartbreaking. Embracing a gypsy life was my future.

Our tiny New York City apartment was one room, a bare tile floor, with two twin beds. Our only window led to the fire escape. Gran's bed was stripped of its sheets, a cold reminder of her passing. The mystery and strangeness of her sudden illness were still on my mind.

Climbing onto the fire escape, I looked up to the sky. The air was cold, but the night was clear, and the full moon and stars were shining. The usual smell of car exhaust was barely noticeable. The horn-honking of taxis seemed faint. There was too much else on my mind. I stood there, deep in thought. A tear ran down my cheek. She was really gone. I couldn't feel her vibrant energy anymore. The chill of the night air invaded my bones. It was nothing compared to the emptiness in my heart.

I slipped back inside and closed the window. The mirror, a simple reflective surface with no frame, was hanging on the wall. It stared back at me. My black hair was thicker and wavier than normal. Gran had always insisted on smoothing out my hair so it would shine. She made special potions for me to help tame it. Since her death, I hadn't bothered. The recipe was in the book. It didn't seem worth it. Was I really that pale? Yes, sadly. My face looked a bit deathly. I shrugged it off. It didn't matter.

My two suitcases, duffle bag, and of course, my electric guitar were sitting there poised, ready for something. For what, I was still unsure. I had no idea where I was going, only that I was leaving. On top of the pile was my grandmother's spellbook, or my book now, I supposed. I traced my finger over the exterior design, the leather binding, the runes engraved in it. They lit up slightly beneath my fingers. This was my family's legacy, the legacy I'd never wanted but now was my life. Gran had been only thirteen when the book came to her. I counted myself lucky that this legacy wasn't solely mine until now, at twenty-seven.

I took in a deep breath and straightened myself out. Where was that damn mail key? Checking that before I left seemed important. More important was to leave a forwarding marker in the box. It would forward any magical messages I might receive. My quest for information to undo the magic on the family spellbook was still a priority. The book contained spells that could do much good, and having it lost to the world was something Gran and I had been working on preventing. Neither of us wanted that to hinge on the continuation of our bloodline. Especially since it ended with relationship-phobic me. I didn't want to lose information from that quest while I was on the road. I found the key and headed down to the box. My neighbor Chris must've heard me on the stairs. He came out of his apartment.

"So uh, Marjorie. Do you want to come by later? Netflix and chill?" He said and winked.

Chris had been a decent distraction in the past, but he was less entertaining as a lover than the movies he picked out. As tempting as mindless sex, in general, might be, his offer wasn't on my agenda.

"Sorry, Chris, I'll have to pass tonight. Going on a trip tomorrow, and much to do. You know the feeling," I said, brushing him off.

I didn't see any point in telling him I was leaving forever. Chris had this delusion for a while that I was his girlfriend. I certainly didn't want to encourage that again. He shrugged, looked disappointed, and then headed back inside.

The apartment mailbox was stuffed with the usual junk mail. I hadn't checked it in a while. Thumbing through the contents, I found a letter addressed to either Gran or me. Our names were both Marjorie Michel, although Gran was usually simply called M. This had always been a joke between us when deciding who opened what mail. Without her, it was only me to see what was inside, regardless of the intended recipient.

Satisfied that no one was around, I quickly drew the needed rune for the marker. Gripping the letter in my hand, I headed back to the apartment to see what it contained. Did I detect a hint of cologne? I made myself comfortable sitting on the bed and opened it. The penmanship was excellent. It was smooth and artistic, and the paper itself had the luxurious texture of the finest stationery.

> *"Dear Marjorie, I hope this letter finds you well. It has been far too long since we have seen each other. I've*

missed your beautiful smile. I find myself in need of aid that may have answers in your famous spell-book. I hope that you will come and see me at the manor and assist me in this dilemma. I also hope to discuss the agreement between our families to determine where you may stand on the matter. I have included a special invite that will guide you here should you accept. I truly have missed your company, and I hope you will take me up on this offer. Love, LZ"

There was a feeling about it that went beyond the mere words on the paper. It had a sense of intimacy. I thought Gran had shunned all relationships, and clearly, this was someone who seemed very fond of her. We'd traveled separately often enough in the past three years. Perhaps this was someone she'd met in her travels? I was surprised she'd never mentioned this person.

Upon examination, the added paper that LZ had called the "invite" was unusual looking, not like anything I'd seen before. It had lettering that was almost glittery but not holographic. It had only two words on the front. "Vernaria," was in large letters at the top, and underneath it said "Ealach." I had no idea what either word meant. The energy pulsing off it was unlike any magic I'd encountered. The instructions on the backside were to be at Grand Central Station tomorrow morning, the very day I'd planned on leaving anyway. This request for help sounded as if it was something Gran would've wanted me to do. It was a call for the book, my legacy, something I couldn't ignore.

I opened the window and went out on the fire escape again, my favorite spot to reflect. I looked up at the moon. I could see

golden sparkles surrounding it; it felt as if they were calling me. No matter the oddity, I had to do this. I had to go.
******

The next morning, I gathered my things, turned in the key, and bid farewell to my landlord. She'd been kind to me, especially in my worst grief stage. We hugged goodbye, and I walked down the street to the subway station.

New snow had fallen, and the wind was the usual biting chill that goes straight to the center of your soul. My admiration for the beauty of the snow wasn't going too well with my outfit. My favorite above-the-knee skirt with tights and knee-high boots was feeling questionable. At least I hadn't been crazy enough to part with my good winter coat. A few people on the subway train looked me over, but they minded their own business like typical New Yorkers.

The subway stop at Grand Central Station was bustling with life as it was on any typical day. Still, it's easy to go unnoticed carting bags through the station. No one tended to look twice at a person carrying their life in tow, not in this city and certainly not at Grand Central.

My heart lifted, hearing the rich sounds of a tenor saxophone echoing against the walls as the man playing offered his smooth rendition of John Legend's "All of Me." A small crowd was surrounding him, enjoying his performance. Others simply walked on. I stopped for a moment to enjoy the song. I wondered when I'd be back in this fantastic city.

As if it was a compass, the paper directed me through the station and to a train platform. I had the invitation in hand, my guitar strapped to my back, and my bags at my side. There was an eerie feeling in the air this far down on the platform. There were far fewer people here. The ones that were seemed entirely lost inside themselves.

The air shifted, and the smell of something burning came through. A black, old-style train pulled up to the platform and stopped. Steam was billowing out of the top. Two other people seemed aware of this train; no one else acted like anything was there. The paper in my hand signaled that this was my ride. A man in a wool uniform jacket with large brass buttons picked up my bags. I never saw him come out of the train, but suddenly he was there. He barely looked at me but went about his business as if only my luggage mattered.

When I boarded, I felt energy scanning my body. I was tingling from head to toe. An odd sense of familiarity rushed over me. How could this be? Did Gran take me here? I had no memory of it, only a feeling.

The interior of the train was lush. The seats were deep crimson, trimmed with golden fabric. Unstrapping my guitar, I slid into a row, putting my case on the seat next to me. There was an unusually thick mist outside the window. It obscured most of what I knew should be there.

The train lurched forward. I could see an outline of buildings through the mist and only a hint of sunlight. Suddenly everything became dark outside the window. It felt as if we entered a long tunnel. My eyes began to feel heavy, and sleep claimed me.

******

"We have arrived, Madam," the attendant informed me as I returned from my deep, dreamless slumber.

"Thank you," I replied, unsure what to say other than that.

He nodded, apparently content that I was awake and ready to disembark. He strolled away with a most unusual gliding to his gait.

I wasn't sure how long I'd been asleep. Minutes? Hours? Outside I could see an outline of trees, but it was pitch black, so the sun had set. A light rain appeared to be falling. I could see some glistening of wet or possibly ice in the tree branches by the light of the partial cloud-obstructed moon.

As I stood up, a piece of paper fell from my lap. It was another letter, or more of a note, not the one I'd initially received.

> *"Thank you, Dear, for coming as requested. I know it may be other than you're accustomed to, but a carriage will be by to collect you and bring you up to the manor. I look forward to seeing you. LZ."*

I began to question my sanity for a moment. Seriously what was I walking into? Was this person going to be upset that I wasn't my grandmother? Would they be distressed that she'd crossed over and they hadn't been notified? Were there to be tears at this news, or simple acceptance? Since this was a magical connection, the stakes could be high. I could be walking into the estate of a powerful, evil witch or wizard. I had some skills, but I wasn't my grandmother. Still, the sense of comfort I kept feeling even amid all the mystery told me this was the right path.

My bags were there on the platform with no sign of an attendant around. The train pulled out of the station smoothly and with little sound even in the stillness of the night.

There was a circle of light cast by the lamp on the platform where I was standing. There were no other people outside, other than the man at the ticket window. With the train's departure, the man went inside a room where a few others were seated around a table. All of them appeared to be in vintage clothing. The entire train station reflected something from the late nineteenth century. At least that was my feeling. Not that historical times were my specialty.

The night air was cold, so I drew my coat tighter around me. Before I could make my way inside, two beautiful black horses appeared, strapped to a carriage; the driver up top was well dressed for the weather in a robust coat with a furry-looking collar and sharp-looking hat on his head. Another man in similar attire appeared and bowed to me.

"M'Lady Marjorie, I presume," he said.

"Yes, I'm Marjorie," I replied

Before I could say another word, he took my luggage and strapped it to the back.

When he opened the carriage door, I stepped inside. The seats were leather, pillowed in texture. In the dim light, they appeared to be either black or a deep red. It was hard to tell. I was feeling a bit like a dark Cinderella in my dark carriage with black horses.

The melodic click of the horse hooves and vibration of the carriage underneath me was oddly soothing. Outside the window, nothing was visible besides shadows. Suddenly the forest cleared. There was a river below and above it a tall hill. The bright moonlight fell upon the silhouette of what appeared to be a formidable-looking structure.

The carriage began its climb up the hill. Suddenly, my mind started racing as a sense of urgency was now mingling with the previous feeling of familiarity. Had I been here before, or was I tapping into some ancestral memory? Or was this merely a spell cast by the mysterious "LZ"?

The closer we got, the friendlier our destination began to look; warm lighting appeared in the windows, a beautifully landscaped garden graced the front. This had to be what LZ had referred to as "the manor." It was clearly the grand home of someone with substantial means.

Because of our unique book, my family was called "royalty" for their expertise in herbal magics, but my grandmother and I were never wealthy. It was a choice she'd made to live more under the radar. She'd been a humble woman who preferred to keep to herself.

Visions began to flow into my head. A blonde girl and a young boy were both laughing, smiling, and running behind a tree. They beckoned me to follow. Another image felt just out of reach, but what I could tell was that it was a sad memory that seemed to pierce my heart. That feeling came through, even if the vision didn't.

Almost there, a sudden fog fell, so thick the manor was no longer visible. It was just ahead, but the fog was so dense even the moonlight was obscured, and we were in pitch black. Even my hand wasn't visible in front of my face.

The horse and driver had to know the route exactly, or we'd be over the cliff. The road leading up to the building had appeared narrow, with one side dropping off into the chasm. Unless, of course, it was only me who was affected, the outsider coming in. It felt like an eternity in that fog, no visions or anything I could see physically. Just black.

Then the carriage stopped. Before I could look out, the door opened. The footman appeared, offering me a hand to step out of the carriage. I stood in front of the manor. The building itself was immense, a grand luxurious home with a sense of immeasurable power. The stone structure looked ancient, but there were more modern-looking sections. It resembled an old castle that had been updated. Not modern, but not medieval.

Standing in front of the door was a tall, handsome, broad-shouldered man. His shoulder-length hair was streaked with white and grey, indicating an age that didn't match the youthful look of his face and skin. He wore a white shirt with large, billowing sleeves and snug-fitting pants that accented his muscular form. Like much of what I'd seen so far on this trip, it suggested an earlier era than modern-day New York City. Had I entered some strange land? A different time? This wasn't Canada, that much I knew.

The man approached the footman, who was carrying my luggage. "Please put these in the West wing, you know which room, I'm sure," he said with a grin on his face. I could see the other man nod and hurry along his way as I approached the door.

"Ah Marjorie, at last. It's so good to see you." He paused as if he was assessing me. His eyes did a scan up and down my body. "Did you bring the book as I requested?"

This greeting dumbfounded me. Did he think I was my grandmother, or was it me he'd been expecting all along? Unsure of what to say, I stood there blinking at him like an idiot. Suddenly he started laughing.

"Oh, this is rich. You don't remember me do you? Not a damn thing. You thought I was writing to your grandmother? I confess I was fond of her, but the letter was only for you."

I could find no words and just kept staring at him, partly because he was so handsome and partly because this was all so confusing. He felt familiar, but the face I couldn't recall at all.

"Come inside with me. We can catch up," he said.

With that, he reached out and touched my hand. With his touch and the view of the great room as we entered, a veil lifted. Memories of laughter and playing in the garden flooded my mind. My head was spinning as I felt bombarded by what felt like an intense download of information. A vision appeared of a younger man with wavy chestnut-brown hair, but it was most certainly the same person. I took a few deep breaths before turning to him again.

"Lazlo! What happened to your hair?"

I blurted this out as his name came accessible in my mind. And his sister, a bubbly blonde.

"Your sister Gwen? Is she here too?"

Now the sensations felt warmer, my heart beating faster with the excitement of the memories. This had been a fun place to be.

He smiled warmly. "I was hoping some memories would be triggered upon entering. As for Gwen, she dwells among the mundane. She gave up her gifts to live a life with neither magic nor estate responsibilities. Her husband and her family are what keep her busy. Relieving her of the estate's binding magic was my wedding gift to her. Now all of the family responsibilities lie with me. The hair, as you pointed out, was a magical side effect."

"Well, you wear it well," I said.

Okay, how dumb did that sound coming out of my mouth?

"Your parents?" I asked.

As more memories were surfacing, I recalled Gran bringing me here. We spent time with him, his sister, and their parents.

"That story's a bit long and complicated. It's better saved for tomorrow after you are rested, but they're no longer here. Gwen departed two years ago, and I've been alone here with my staff ever since. Your grandmother was one of my occasional visitors in recent years. She never brought you, though, not since the two of you disappeared."

My entire body was tingling as he took my hand and pressed his lips against the back of it. The sensation was heavenly. When he raised his eyes to meet mine, that sensation intensified. His eyes themselves were magical, a blue-green color with flecks of violet. There was a hint of sadness too, but also a love of life behind them. In that instant, I wanted him more than I've ever wanted a man in my life. He smiled, almost as if that thought had been shared, or at least that was my imagination. Instantly I flushed, embarrassed at that possibility.

I took a step back, out of his intoxicating space. "In answer to your previous question, yes, I brought the book. It's with me always. It's my legacy."

Composing myself around him was going to prove difficult.

He nodded. "Good. Tomorrow we can get to work. For now, my lovely Marjorie, it's late, and I'm sure you must be exhausted from your trip. I'll have Roland bring you some tea - and let him know if you need any food as well. He will show you to your room."

With that, Lazlo offered a polite bow at the waist and withdrew.

I still felt flushed, hot, and bothered by that intense energy of being in his space. Roland led me silently up a stairway and down a hall.

Why didn't Gran bring me here with her on those more recent trips? What had happened to my memory? I'd been aware of what felt like missing pieces, but whenever I brought this up, Gran had always filled the gaps. Now I was beginning to suspect there was much of my life I couldn't remember, and that many of my memories had been manufactured by my grandmother. But why?

The curve of the wood on the four-post bed was familiar. I knew I'd been here before. Memories of the three of us coming in here playing, looking out the window, laughing, then Gran was shooing us out. Oh, how I missed her.

There was a beautiful dressing gown hanging inside the room. It was a shimmering deep green in color—nothing fancy, just pretty.

"Who does this belong to?" I inquired of Roland as he was turning down the bed.

"Master Lazlo had that brought in for you to wear if you please," he said.

His polite smile indicated he liked the idea himself. Was he flirting with me? I ignored it.

"Thank you, Roland, and no need to bring anything. I'm fine."

Once Roland left me, I took in my surroundings. It was dark, and the view from the window was mostly shadows. Still, under the moonlight, there was a hint that the morning view would be spectacular.

Undressing for bed, I couldn't resist trying on that pretty gown. The fabric was soft and luxurious against my skin. It felt so sensual. I lay on the bed, intending to change again, but before I could think another thought, I felt myself drifting into a deep sleep.

The Proposal

I was in the hallway and knocked on a nearby door. The door opened to reveal Lazlo, shirtless. His perfectly sculpted chest glistened with a hint of sweat. Royal blue silk pajama pants were hanging loosely on his narrow hips. I dropped my dressing gown to the floor and stood naked in front of him. He pulled me in close. His grip was tight, deliberate. Our lips met in a passionate kiss as his hands fell to my hips, bringing our lower bodies to touch. My body was on fire with the yearning to have him. He pulled me into his arms and threw me onto the bed. He climbed on top of me as I opened myself fully to him and invited him into me, our energies pulsing together. My body was glowing, as was his from our magical energetic exchange.

Sex dreams can be so satisfying. Once I knew I had total control of the dream, I dreamed of sex with him in different positions and variations. Each time the connection delivered a massive load of energy through me, leaving me feeling supercharged. After a night of enormous satisfaction, the dream slipped away.

******

I awoke in the bed just as I'd drifted off the night before. My entire body still felt magically charged. I checked myself.

I was still wearing clothes. My body didn't feel as if I'd physically engaged anyone. A sense of relief washed over me. For a moment, I feared my dream sense had been wrong, that I'd done something inappropriate. Lazlo had a job to accomplish, and while I wasn't sure what that was yet, I was certain my dream behavior wasn't going to help either of our goals. Besides, this morning when I met with Lazlo, those lustful feelings surely would vanish. My dream version was unlikely to match up to the real man.

A note brought in from Roland invited me to join Lazlo downstairs for breakfast. The man was clearly a fan of letters and notes. I found it charming. Dressing in the same outfit I'd been wearing the night before seemed the sanest solution. I was in no mood to rifle through my bags to find something else just yet.

When I arrived downstairs, Lazlo was in the dining room. To my surprise, he was wearing the same silk pajama pants from my dream. They were hanging seductively on his hips, clinging to him in ways that didn't leave much to the imagination. He was wearing a robe, but it was open. Between his exposed chest and the nature of those pants, it was difficult not to stare. As exciting as he was, he was also a bit intimidating.

He smiled as he reached for his cup of tea off a nearby serving tray.

"Did you sleep well, Marjorie?"

An involuntary heat rose in my skin. It was embarrassing to be asked that by the subject of the seductive dreams I'd enjoyed while I slept.

"Yes, thank you, did you?" I asked.

He grinned and moved in close to me, his face inches from mine. I could feel the heat of his body. His closeness was uncomfortable. Still, I hesitated to move away.

"Honestly, not so well, but you know what they say. . . if you can't sleep, you're awake in someone else's dream," he said. His eyes sparkled playfully as his hand reached to slip a stray curl of my hair behind my ear.

"Your hair is so different now. I like this look on you. And that little skirt. I've never seen a woman dressed like that," he said, glancing at my legs. "It's quite charming—apologies for my own attire. I didn't expect you down here so quickly, or I'd be more appropriately dressed," he said before allowing his hand to gently glide down my arm as he took a step away. His eyes remained fixed on me.

"Apology accepted," I said, attempting to sound cool.

I took another step back, determined to maintain my own sense of power. How was he even more enticing in person than he'd been in that dream?

"So," I said, taking a deep breath to recompose myself, "why'd you ask me here?"

He motioned for me to take a seat at the table. He walked over and moved the chair out. Roland brought over some warm coffee, tea, and an array of different foods.

"Your grandmother was good enough to let me know a bit about the quest the two of you were pursuing," he said as he seated himself at the table. "However, she never informed me of your memory loss. I assumed you weren't interested in coming to see me these past years."

"I admit I'm a bit confused by the memory loss. I don't know why Gran kept this from me." I said.

"Nor do I. The last message I received from her was about how to contact you. I was surprised, to say the least. I decided that was my cue to reach out to you. Seeing you now, how enchanting you still are, I'm even more glad that I made that choice."

It wasn't that I was unaccustomed to men complimenting or coming on to me, but this felt different. I was unsure of his intentions or interest.

"So then, Gran told you of our quest to break the curse on my family book. That we don't want it to disappear forever if there isn't a magically inclined blood relative to accept it." I said

"Yes, and it seems that you have several options. You can, of course, remove that spell, but I hope you are examining the potential consequences of that book being able to find itself in the hands of just anyone." he turned to Roland and gestured to him. Roland removed a few things off the table, bowed, and exited the room. Lazlo turned back to me. He was smooth, comfortable, confident, and fascinating. Who was this man? "Another option, of course, you may have all but exhausted, is to confirm the existence of another blood relative with the ability to attract the book. Of course, your other alternative is to continue your family line," he said, leaning back into his chair slightly.

Once again, I found myself avoiding his eyes. "You're correct," I said, choosing to look at the assortment of food instead of him. "Gran and I were both searching for relatives and couldn't find any with a spark of magic in them. As for me, well, even if I did bear a child, it might not have the magical ability. So, I'd rather not. Removing the spell has been my focus, but thanks for that additional insight. It does contain spells and formulas that could do a lot of harm in the wrong hands."

"Well, you might consider casting a new spell on it, one

requiring some integrity of the user or some such thing," he said. Even his deep baritone voice was appealing. This man was absolutely everything I found attractive.

I nodded. "So what about you? Why did you ask me here." I dared a look back up at him.

"Well, since Gwen abdicated, I hold the status and power of the family as well as, similar to you, the responsibility to continue it." He leaned across the table. His gaze was mesmerizing, and I wanted to get lost in it.

"And to that end, I thought it might benefit us both . . ."

Something in his manner triggered me. Hadn't I just said that wasn't what I wanted?

"Stop right there, mister. You so did not invite me on that weird train ride out here in the middle of nowhere just to bed me and breed with me!"

Lazlo backed away in his chair, rising up straight and tall as though somewhat offended.

" Honestly, Marjorie, no, that was not my intention, nor was it what I meant. The truth is, I had hoped you would remember what we shared. You seem unable to recall the relationship we had."

"Relationship?" I asked.

"Yes," he said. There was a hint of frustration in his voice. "My parents agreed to a marriage contract at my request. My mother was happy enough at the idea of joining our families, and you and your grandmother also agreed to it. Technically we are promised to each other." he said.

"Wait. What? You're saying I'm engaged to you?" I felt a tightness in my throat at that thought.

"Yes, that's another way of saying it."

He took a casual sip of his tea as if this idea was completely normal to him. My head was spinning. This felt so bizarre.

"No offense, but I haven't even seen you in what - ten years or more? Add to that, I don't even remember most of my time here nor much about you. We agreed to this when exactly? When I was how old?" I asked, my voice nearly squeaking in my panic. I tended to stay away from relationships in general. Marriage was practically a phobia for me.

His eyes met mine. I could sense him contemplating my terror mixed with anger.

"Apologies. That part of my letter must have been confusing. The original contract between our families was drawn up when I was seventeen, and you were fifteen, after... well, you don't remember, so it isn't important."

"But it's important to you, isn't it?" I asked.

He shrugged, dismissing the question.

"It wasn't long afterwards that the two of you disappeared. I was, admittedly, rather confused. As far as I knew, you and I were on good terms. No one could find you. My letters couldn't reach you."

"You sent me letters?"

"Yes, but they all came back. Then three years ago, your grandmother showed up here. She stressed our time apart and your need to make your own choices. I made her a gentleman's agreement that should I see you again, I wouldn't press the issue."

He paused, looking across the table at me as if waiting for a response. I wondered what had happened. Had I gotten cold feet and Gran helped me run away? Then why the memory loss?

"What do you mean by pressing the issue? Gran didn't explain any of this to me."

"All I mean is that if you want to join with me, I'm happy to have you. If not… I respect that decision as well. I do hope you'll consider it."

"Consider marrying you? From an agreement that was reached when we were teenagers?"

"Yes. There's no need for an immediate answer. Please learn all you need to learn first. We were close once, you and I. Very close." He paused, looking at me for a moment as if he was assessing me. "Regardless of your decision on that matter, I hope you'll continue the work your grandmother was aiding me with."

"Which was what, exactly?" I asked

"I want to find a way to seal or dismantle our ancestral gate, to send those souls inside to where they belong instead of leaving them trapped in limbo. Then none from my lineage will be shackled to this estate. So you see, our goals are not so different."

"Your ancestral gate? My grandmother told me folk tales about a legendary ring of souls. Is that the same thing?"

He nodded. "Yes. It's a container that holds the spirits of my ancestors. My family draws additional power from it."

"So what if I can't help. What if we can't figure out how to do that?"

"Well, if we find no solutions for me other than to stay bound to this estate, I'll need to marry and continue the family. If not you, then another," he said.

"So what if we succeed? Then what?" I asked.

"Then I'll be able to go where I want when I want. The marriage part loses its importance with regards to family responsibilities. Then it becomes more of a union between two people who simply desire it," he said.

"So even if we can do that, I mean close this gate, your proposal is still valid? You'd still want to marry some chick you haven't seen in over a decade?"

His eyes met mine; they were captivating. He smiled and said, "Perhaps."

I had to look away from those eyes. Looking down at that bare chest was not the best option, however. Fuck, he was way too hot. Did he notice I was staring? My eyes drifted back up to his face. Yep, he noticed. My skin felt hot; it had to be red. Lazlo stood up from the table.

"Well, Marjorie, if you've no objections, I'll go get dressed, and then let's take a look at that book of yours and see what notes your grandmother had in there. Roland will escort you to the study. I'll join you there shortly."

With that, he departed. My head was still whirling as I attempted to process all of this new information. Engaged? At fifteen? It sounded so bizarre. Then again, this wasn't the modern-day world I'd been living in. Things were done differently here.

Once I finished breakfast, Roland led me down a short hallway into a neighboring room. Bookshelves lined two of the walls. There was a desk, a table, and a few chairs. A fireplace was at one end with a small couch and a couple of overstuffed armchairs. I had a strange feeling of another presence.

"Roland, is there anyone else here? Besides you, Lazlo, and the other staff members?"

"No, M'am. We are the only people here," he said.

I shook off the strange feeling and signaled that it was okay for him to leave me. Still, something was odd here. I couldn't quite decipher it. I sat down at the desk and began flipping through pages in my book, looking for Gran's notes.

It wasn't long before Lazlo came strolling across the study. In his gray shirt with a black buttoned-up vest and jacket, he was still a striking figure. But thankfully, less exposed, he wasn't as distracting. Some memories of the boy I'd been friends with were resurfacing, but they contrasted greatly with the dashing man he'd grown into. It was a bit dizzying, all of this new information, but I was doing my best to process it.

"Hello, Marjorie," he said as he sat down next to me. He was a bit more generous with personal spacing this time, but still, he was intoxicating to be near.

"Hi again," I said. "Um, so, you haven't told me yet how you ended up here alone. What happened to your parents?"

Lazlo looked away, staring at the wall as if deep in thought for a moment.

"As I said last night, it's a bit of a complex tale. One day Mother announced that they needed to go on a trip. Just her and Father. It would fall to Gwen and myself to keep the gate balanced in their absence." His gaze shifted downward. "We assumed it was some sort of getaway to repair their marriage. What we didn't know was before she left, Mother had become possessed by one of our ancestral spirits."

Lazlo stood up and walked to the other side of the table. He paused, thumbing through one of the journals.

"They never returned. From what we heard, my mother likely murdered my father and still roams out there today," he said strolling over to look out the window. I couldn't imagine what that felt like, the idea that one of your parents murdered the other.

"So, have you been able to find out anything at all since then?" I asked.

He turned back to me. "Before Gwen left, I took a few

pilgrimages to find Mother, but I came up cold. Since then, however, I've been unable to leave here to try to find her."

"Why can't you leave?" He'd mentioned keeping the gate balanced, but I was curious why that was so important.

"Duty to the safety of others, primarily. The ancestors behind that gate are powerful and can be dangerous. If the gate isn't maintained with the proper rituals, we risk the malevolent spirits getting out, past the boundaries of this estate, and causing damage to others. We have to keep that from happening."

"So basically, you're telling me that your mother is still alive but inhabited by an evil spirit?"

"Sadly yes, and likely gaining power," Lazlo said.

"Not all of us are bad!" said a strange voice from out of nowhere.

I let out a squeal, startled at the sight of an apparition hovering next to Lazlo.

"Samoth, what did I tell you about frightening our guest?" Lazlo said, scolding the ghostly form.

"But you can't let her think we're all evil. That wouldn't be right." Samoth objected.

"Apologies, Marjorie." Lazlo said, returning to his seat next to me, "I should've warned you earlier. I allow a few of the ancestral spirits to wander parts of the manor. They are, like Samoth, not at all a threat and nothing to be frightened of."

"They aren't, you know, in the bedrooms or anything, are they?" I leaned in and whispered to Lazlo. Suddenly the idea of some pervert ghost watching me undress was unsettling.

"No, they're not. The only eyes in that part of the manor belong to the living," he whispered back, clearly amused by my reaction.

"I only go where Master Lazlo so graciously allows me to go. Those of us allowed are thankful for his generosity," the ghost added.

Lazlo shrugged at the ghost's compliment. "The troubling part is that inside that ring, beyond the gate, they all reside. Some are decent souls like Samoth here, and others are truly terrifying. And though he still is too afraid to tell me which spirit is riding inside Mother, I keep hoping he'll find the strength to tell me."

"I'm sorry, Master Lazlo, you didn't see what he did, how he tore other spirits apart."

The idea that a ghost - someone already dead - feared something was undoubtedly unsettling.

"Yes, you did tell me about that, just as I have asked you to stop calling me Master. I thank you for even that information about what we may have to deal with. Once I find a way to release spirits entirely, you'll be at the top of the list to finally get to your afterlife. For now, please leave us."

The apparition offered a slight bow and floated away. This was all so weird.

"Geez, anything else you want to confess to? I mean, it seems you've got your fair share of issues to work out," I suddenly blurted out.

Lazlo laughed. "You're right. It's a lot. So knowing all of this, are you willing to help me? If we can balance the gate enough, I can leave here for a more extended time and go after Mother. I need your research to see if your book has any answers to help me."

"Okay, it's all a bit weird, and I'm not sure what I can do, but I'm on board to continue what Gran started. So what do you know about this spirit that escaped and is parading around in your mother's body?"

"So far, not that much. You saw how frightened Samoth was. The list can be narrowed to the more terrifying of my ancestors. Sadly, that isn't a shortlist. Which reminds me, I must take leave of you and see to my daily tasks in that area." he said, rising from his seat. "Are you alright here on your own? I can send Roland down if you like."

"Thank you, I'm fine."

He nodded and turned away. I watched him as he walked out of the room. I wondered what my life might have been like had Gran and I never left this realm.

An Unexpected Discovery

I turned to the bookshelf to see what might be of aid besides Gran's notes. To have any chance of succeeding, I needed to know more about this family, about their history and their magic.

"I'd suggest this one," a ghostly hand appeared with the voice. It pointed to a large, leather-bound book. The rest of the shape of a woman appeared through the bookcase. I steadied myself from the startle it gave me. This would take some getting used to.

"Thank you," I replied, pulling the book off the shelf. "What's your name?" If the ghost was friendly enough to point me in the right direction, perhaps she'd share some information as well.

"Franshia is what I was called. Logically if you are here to help release us, you are seeking information about the original spell that created the gate. That book contains much of the information."

"Franshia, where do you fit in the lineage? I mean, what is your relation to Lazlo? How far back do these ancestors go?"

"I am one of the newer inhabitants. I was Lazlo's grandmother, the last matriarch of this household before my daughter, who currently holds that position."

"But she ran off, didn't she? So where does that leave Lazlo?"

"My darling grandson is in limbo. He's not fully in charge here and cannot be unless that power is handed to him by his mother. Or upon her death. With the abdication of his sister, he holds tremendous power but still only a percentage of his mother's."

"I don't suppose you've told Lazlo which ancestor escaped?"

"One very dark and ancient is all I can say. Like Samoth, I do not wish to be shredded across the realms for eternity should it return and realize my betrayal through the bond we spirits share."

"That does sound awful. So if Lazlo is successful in releasing you, what does that mean for him?"

"A loss of substantial power, although he is quite gifted without it. Thankfully a lust for power is not in my grandson's heart. He's a kind soul, more like his father. He'll make someone an excellent husband."

She paused, giving me a once-over. Her affection for Lazlo was apparent; I didn't know how to respond other than to smile at her.

She floated over the nearby desk. "Most of us trapped here only thought about the power, about duties, never about the torment the poor souls were suffering until we became one of them. Lazlo is different. He can see beyond power."

"So, if we're successful, then Lazlo never becomes a trapped soul?"

"Exactly, our entire lineage would be free of this curse. More I cannot tell you in the detail that you need, but that book contains much information you will find helpful."

Franshia departed as suddenly as she'd appeared. I wondered if I was truly alone now. This place was strange indeed.

When opening the book, the aura coming from it shocked me. It matched that of my own spell-book. The individual who had cast the conditions on my book was involved in creating the gate in this manor that bound the spirits.

Checking Gran's notes, I was surprised to learn that she knew this already. The mage was Maximillien, an ancestor of Ealach. This was the same wizard who'd also cast the curse on the book that Gran said killed my mother. We'd been searching for information on him to release our spell-book. Supposedly no one knew precisely who that mage was or where he came from. But Gran, she knew all of it and never told me.

The more I read, the more frightening it became. The darkest of magic was used to create this gate. Souls had been pulled forth from the other side and tricked before trapping them. Maximillien chose the most powerful of his ancestors, bound them to their bloodline. The curse, of course, claimed Maximillien himself upon his own death.

I rechecked Gran's notes. There was a potential solution, more research was needed, but this could work if I could find one more element. I must have been lost in my reading when Roland startled me by tapping on my shoulder.

"M'Lady, Master Lazlo is requesting that you join him for dinner. Perhaps you would like to change into some dinner clothes?"

"I'm sorry, Roland, but what do you mean by dinner clothes?" I asked. I suddenly wondered if I hadn't packed appropriately for this visit. There was nothing particularly dressy in my bags.

"I believe there is a change hanging in your room for you right now, M'Lady," Roland said.

Back in my room, hanging in front of the closet was a

beautiful crimson gown. Dressing like this was certainly not something I was used to. This luxurious dress seemed over the top for any dinner I'd ever attended. Well, "when in Rome," right? The fabric felt lightweight in my hands, smooth and silky. I stepped into it. As I pulled it up, the dress conformed to my figure, clinging seductively. The bust-line was lower than I'd have chosen. I felt a bit exposed, but it looked fantastic. I styled my hair into a half updo, allowing the back to fall free. I felt deserving of compliments and attention. I felt like royalty.

When I walked into the dining room, he stood as I entered. Like a prince in a fairy tale, he was elegantly dressed. His hair was tied back in a ponytail. His long jacket was a deep blue velvet with gold trim and gold buttons; underneath was a black and gray vest and a white shirt. There was already food on the table, but there was no sign of Roland or any staff. We were alone.

"Apologies for not rejoining you this afternoon. I had much to attend to. It took longer than I'd planned." he said with a polite bow.

He walked over and pulled out a chair, motioning for me to take a seat.

"No apology necessary. I've lots to discuss with you, however, after my research." I said, taking the seat he offered.

"Let's let that wait until after dinner, shall we? I've had enough of my family history for now." He moved my chair toward the table. " I'd like to enjoy some time together, to reacquaint ourselves. I think you'll agree we've plenty catching up to do. To start, I must say, you look beautiful in that gown. Your previous outfit was lovely, but I thought you might enjoy something different for tonight, after all your travels and studies. A reminder of how things are in Vernaria, or at least here at Ealach Manor."

He took his seat at the table. His scan up and down my body felt like a lover's caress, and it was only with his eyes. I squirmed a bit in my seat. Part of me was longing to be laid across the dinner table or bent over it while he thrust himself into me. I wanted to torment him, to seduce him. At the same time, I desperately wanted *not* to want him at all.

He bit his lip and fixed his eyes on mine. "Marjorie, I can sense some of those thoughts, and they are quite distracting. The image flash is a bit much if I'm to continue to give you the space requested, rather than openly courting you. Out of curiosity, how long has it been since you've acted on that impulse?" he asked. His tone was controlled and casual as if he'd simply asked what I had for breakfast.

My entire exposed flesh went scarlet with embarrassment. I was unaware of how magic worked here and felt like I'd been caught and sent to the Principal's office.

Suddenly I couldn't help but start laughing. Lazlo smiled and chuckled in response but looked confused.

"I'm delighted to see that smile and hear you laugh, but what is so funny?" he asked.

"Is this truly your idea of casual dinner conversation? Talking about my sex life? And why are men always so curious about that?"

He laughed again. "What can I say? I like to know what my challenges are, particularly if you decide I'm at least allowed to court you. It tends to help me win," he said. His eyes carried a sense of play in them, teasing me about my responses. He paused, sat back, and looked at me. "I sense that you don't know how amazing you are. You are absolutely riveting."

I rolled my eyes. "What wouldn't you say to get the nearest

available woman to your bed. I know a playboy when I see one."

"Playboy? I admit to liking the company of women, but I'm unsure of that reference. I wouldn't compliment a woman if I didn't mean it, and I assure you no strings are attached to my compliments. I'm an honest man Marjorie, even if I was admittedly at times a bit of a brat as a child, I was never a liar."

I laughed again. "Yes, the longer I'm here, the more I remember that mischievous boy and see him again in your eyes. Which, in fact, causes me to question your motives. You are accustomed to getting your way."

He shrugged slightly. "True enough. I am, and I do, quite often. Although lately, it isn't as if I've faced major challenges. You, however, often challenged me. I've missed that, even if I didn't always win."

He flashed a playful smile. I started laughing again, and he joined, neither of us sure what we were laughing about.

Suddenly, in that moment of laughter amid all of this strangeness, our connection felt genuine. I remembered more of a feeling. Lazlo had been a friend, someone I'd treasured. I couldn't remember details, but that feeling was coming through.

Roland entered the dining room with a young man I hadn't seen before. The younger man looked terribly nervous. Roland stood aside and directed him as more food was set on the table. Lazlo turned to the young man.

"Thank you, Maro, I believe we are fine for now. Is Roland treating you well?" His eyes shifted to Roland who smiled.

"Yes Sir, very well. Thank you, Sir," Maro replied with a bow.

Lazlo nodded and the two men left the room. He turned to me.

"It's his first day here. He's Roland's nephew," he explained.

"Are all of your staff related?"

"Not all of them, but some. I keep a minimal staff presently. I offered to retain everyone, but most opted to move on once it was only me here."

"Was there someone here named Charles? That name is coming into my head but I'm not sure."

"Yes, Charles had Roland's position for many years. He retired three summers ago. I still see him occasionally when I go to town."

"Didn't you get in trouble with him a lot?"

He laughed. "Oh, yes. I was quite tiring to poor Charles for many years."

Lazlo and I continued to reminisce as we enjoyed dinner. Certain details were resurfacing in my mind as we talked. I sensed a reluctance on Lazlo's part to share a piece of his memories. He was holding back something. Everything we were discussing was years prior to the time that felt like a blank space if I attempted to remember.

"You haven't said anything about the last time I was here, the time I don't remember at all. Why?" I finally asked.

"It seems impolite. You don't remember. Nothing I say will change that," he said.

"What makes you so sure?" I asked.

He shrugged. "If that dress you're wearing didn't trigger any memories, then the loss was manufactured, deliberate. I lack the power to revive it," he said.

"This dress? What's it got to do with anything?"

"It's *your* dress. You left it here. I was curious if it would trigger any additional memories. Clearly, it did not."

"No way! Gran would never have let me wear this. Not at

fifteen."

He smiled. "Well, the first time I saw you in it, there was a white piece," he gestured to his chest, "making it more, well, modest," he said.

I rolled my eyes. "That sounds like Gran. Did you take that out, then?" I asked.

"No, that was you. When your grandmother was away, you decided to wear it the way you wanted," he said with a smile.

"That does sound like something I'd do."

"And you remember none of this, do you?" he asked.

"No. It's pretty frustrating."

"Then I say we start fresh. No need to frustrate you further. Perhaps our recent lives?"

In that spirit, he shifted the conversation. He talked about the nearest village and local events that had been of interest to him. I shared a few insights about life in New York City. He seemed fascinated.

As we were winding down dinner, Roland once again appeared. He and Lazlo exchanged some words. Lazlo stood up from the table.

"Shall we move to the drawing-room? You can share with me all you've learned in your research," he said as he moved my chair out and gave me his hand.

He led me into the nearby drawing-room. Inside were plush chairs, a small sofa, and a few delicately beaded lamps. There was a fire burning in the fireplace. I took a seat in one of the chairs in front of the fire. Lazlo seated himself in another chair next to me.

"So, tell me about your research," he said.

"Well, there's something I must tell you and something I must ask you," I said.

"Anything," he said. His voice was difficult not to find seductive even if he swore he wasn't trying to sway me.

"Between Gran's notes and what I discovered today, I think I'm close to figuring out how to close that gate. But only the spirits on the other side will be able to cross over. Any spirit left on this side is trapped here."

"That is splendid news. I need to be out there to find my mother and bring her back here. What little I know about that spirit inhabiting Mother is enough to tell me we don't want it out in the world."

"Agreed. So my goal now is to find a way to balance it for longer so that you can travel, at least a bit," I said.

"So that's what you're telling me. What is it that you need to ask me? I'm an open book, ready to tell you whatever you want to know."

"Funny that you mentioned a book. Your grandmother's spirit guided me to a book. It carried a distinct aura of one spelled by the same magician that cast the original spell on our family tome," I said.

"Yes, it would. The spell on your book was cast by one of my ancestors. Your grandmother knew this. That's why she showed up here three years ago. She wanted information we had here regarding that spell. " Lazlo said.

I was still surprised that Gran knew this and never told me. She'd told me plenty of legends but conveniently left this knowledge out.

"What's confusing is that the legends I encountered said that spell caster was a slave to a powerful mage. How did a family of slaves create wealth like this?" I asked.

"Oh, he wasn't a slave; he was a prisoner. He murdered a young girl from a powerful family. His mother was horrified at the potential backlash and turned him in. Eventually, he was hanged for cursing books he was writing while in prison. The havoc those books continue to cause is why we keep the fact that he is our ancestor a bit of a closely guarded secret," he said.

"Those would be the famous time-curse books, right?" I asked. Those particular books each possessed a unique curse. It didn't activate until a certain number of people had read it. The person who read it when the time had run out was doomed. According to Gran, this was how my mother died.

"Yes, terribly sneaky curses. They've done much damage. If my grandmother guided you, then you also know he created the gate. Or was part of its creation."

"So basically, you're saying that ripping souls from behind the veil of death and trapping them to gain power was okay with your family, but they drew the line at the murder of the living when it was a person of some power?"

"True, I never said my ancestors were all lovely people."

"Yes, you indicated many of them were quite the opposite."

He nodded in agreement before looking as if he was temporarily lost in thought.

"Well, Marjorie, is that all for now?"

"I think so. I'll continue digging tomorrow."

"Then, I fear I must take my leave of you for tonight and attend to some matters. You certainly have given me much to think about."

His eyes gazed into mine.

"Roland will assist you with any needs you may have. My apologies for not having female staff other than my cook. I trust you do not require assistance in and out of clothing. If you do, please let Roland know, and he will ask her to assist you."

From out of nowhere, I leaned over and kissed him. It was just a quick kiss, but it certainly got his attention. He stopped, looked at me, and took a deep breath.

I could feel my hands trembling slightly. Had I opened a door? I wasn't sure if he would ignore it or move on it, and I was nervous either way. Lazlo smiled gently, stood up, offered a slight bow, then turned and walked away.

The Magic Man

The next morning I went down to the dining room for breakfast. There was no sign of Lazlo. Food was laid out, and there were beverages, but no one was there. I poked my head in the kitchen to see Roland and Beatrice, the cook, seated at a table chatting.

"Roland, where's Lazlo?"

Roland stood immediately when he saw me. "He sends his apologies, M'Lady. He told me to tell you he'd see you at dinner this evening, but not likely before."

"Did he say why?" I asked.

"He went into town early this morning. He had business he was attending to, as he normally does."

"So being here all day isn't what he normally does?"

"No, M'Lady, he has many responsibilities. But don't worry, we are here to assist you should you need us."

Beatrice smiled and nodded in agreement.

"Thank you both for that. Do you mind if I join you here? I'd feel a bit strange out there all by myself."

Beatrice piped up. "Of course you can!"

Roland went out into the dining room and brought in the food he'd laid out there. They were both friendly and welcoming. It felt good to have people to talk to. Still, I worried if I'd actually driven Lazlo away. Was it partly because of me he wasn't here?

For the next few days, Lazlo remained mostly absent. He showed up for dinner, was friendly, and we shared some laughs. Other than that, he was nowhere to be found.

I continued to learn about this strange place. As I suspected, electricity as I knew it was non-existent here. Everything that lit up did so with magic. The electronic devices I'd brought with me weren't much use for note-taking.

I spent my days in various libraries and studies, taking notes the old-fashioned way. Franshia was oddly coming to feel like a friend-if one can develop a friendship with a ghost. Samoth, on the other hand, may have been well-intentioned but typically ended up being rather useless. It was stories of his life that he enjoyed sharing. He was droning on when I read something intriguing. I looked up to process the thought.

"Marjorie dear, what have you discovered ?" Franshia inquired. She was keen on gaining information and typically watched me closely.

"What do you know about the amulet that was supposed to be Gwen's? Does she still have it?" I asked.

"That I cannot tell you. It was a device of Gwen's creation. Since she gave up her power, it is unlikely she took it with her. I'm not allowed in that area of the manor, so whether or not it's in her old room, I cannot say."

From what I'd read in Maeve's notes, this amulet was an amplifier. It could be helpful to aid Lazlo, although very little of its actual properties were listed other than stating it was limited in use to female family members. It was possible that, if placed correctly with some natural magic, the amulet could balance the gate for an extended period of time. It also was likely it might be useful in the end game of gaining the added power needed to dismantle the gate entirely.

Roland showed me to Gwen's old room. After a thorough search, I came up empty-handed. It seemed my only option would be to seek out Gwen herself and see what answers she could provide. I was hopeful she could tell me how to manipulate it for use outside the family since I wasn't finding anything in the notes. I'd have to corner Lazlo, distant as he was being, and get him to talk to me, other than just over dinner, if I was going to find her.

Roland came in to check on me to inquire if I needed anything.

"Roland, there is something you can help me with," I said.

He nodded. "Of course, M'Lady. What can I do for you?"

"I'd like an audience with Lazlo after dinner tonight. Can you tell him for me? It feels like it would be a more formal request going through you, rather than me hunting him down and asking him."

Roland's eyes lit up. I knew he was dying for Lazlo and I to get together.

"It would be my pleasure, M'Lady," Roland said.

As soon as he left, my nerves were on fire. Doubts trickled in. I shifted them aside. Of course he'd agree. We were friends, right? Our dinner conversations had seemed friendly, at least.

After finishing up my notes, I went to my room to decide what to wear for dinner. I'd adopted the habit of dressing up as if it were an event, especially since it was the only time I was seeing Lazlo. He'd been generous enough to provide an interesting wardrobe for me to choose from. Even if I wasn't sure I wanted to be his bride, so much of me still wanted him to want me. The cooler he got, the more I wanted him.

Roland knocked at the door. He handed me a note. He was grinning. This man had no poker face, and I found it adorable. I opened the note.

"My apologies Marjorie but I will be absent for dinner tonight. However, please meet me in the study afterwards. I will be there. It will be my pleasure to see you and discuss whatever it is you have on your mind."

When I entered the study, he was seated by the fireplace. He was clothed in his usual form-fitting pants, a loose, slightly open shirt, and dark maroon jacket. He had a drink in his hand. He smiled and stood as I walked into the room.

"Come, sit with me," he said. He motioned for me to join him on the small divan. My heart was racing as I sat next to him, our thighs touching on the small sofa. Fuck, why did he affect me like this?

"So tell me, what is it that you have on your mind?" he said. He put an arm around me to make room next to his broad shoulders. The heat of his body so close to mine was exhilarating. With all the things I'd hoped to talk with him about, reconnect with him, tell him about, what came out of my mouth was not what I planned at all.

"You," was all I said. I looked up at his eyes and had to avert mine quickly.

He looked slightly surprised at that. "You've certainly been on my mind as well. I've had much to think about. But what is on your mind that needed this discussion tonight?" he asked.

What was wrong with me? Why did I say that?

"I'm sorry, I don't know what I was thinking, interrupting your routine." I started to get up, embarrassed that I'd even asked him here.

He grabbed my arm, stopping me. The feeling of his flesh on mine, that firm grip sent shockwaves to the core of my being. What was it about him?

"It's no bother. I'm happy to be here for whatever you need. I'm your host, and I want to make myself available to my guest. Please sit and talk to me."

I looked back at him. So many emotions were rushing through me. I thought I had it all under control, and now here he was, in this somewhat romantic attire and this rather romantic setting, in front of a beautiful fireplace.

I sat back down. Perhaps this wasn't my initial plan, but it had been on my mind.

"I've been thinking. I mean, I want us to understand things about each other," I said.

"Well, Marjorie, you've made it clear you aren't ready to accept my proposal. I understand that, and I'm respecting your boundaries just as I promised I would. If you *have* decided you have an answer for me, I will respect it no matter what it is."

My heart was beating faster. I couldn't deny my fierce attraction to him.

"I appreciate that very much, but no, I don't have an answer. But, I've been wondering if my boundaries, as you say, are keeping us from, well keeping me from seeing, what might be possible."

He was silent, looking at me.

"So, I guess what I'm asking, what I'm curious about, is if we take away the big picture, don't worry about the future, then what do you want right now?" I asked.

This was not the conversation I'd intended, but at the moment, it felt necessary. I had a burning need to know. Did he want me even if I hadn't made a decision to be his bride?

He smiled. His hand traced my forehead, lifting a strand of hair behind my ear. I couldn't look away from his eyes.

"If you are asking me to be completely honest, then at this moment, I want what I've wanted from the moment you stepped out of that carriage and back into my life. Right now, I would love to kiss you." He paused, keeping his eyes on mine. Was that heat from the fire or just between us?

I placed my hand on his thigh and slid closer to him. He pulled me in tightly, his arms wrapping around me as he pressed his lips against mine. It was a simple kiss, but it left me longing for more.

"Is this what you want, Marjorie?" he whispered as he pulled away slightly.

I grabbed the collar of his jacket, pulling him back to me and bringing my lips to his. My lips parted inviting his tongue to dance with mine. His mouth tasted slightly of the whiskey he'd been drinking. Even that was turning me on. It felt as if something was unlocking, allowing me to let go of my fears. I felt lost in the moment, lost in my desire for him. His hand slid into the top of my dress and cupped my breast. His grip intensified, just rough enough to excite me further. He kissed down my neck, across my chest. I moaned in delight.

"You feel divine," he managed through his breath as his hands caressed me.

"I want you," I whispered in his ear, allowing my hand to slide further up his thigh and rest between his legs.

His eyes shifted to my hand, then back up to meet mine. "Would you like to take this to your room?" He said softly, a smile forming on his lips.

I nodded. "Yes, absolutely"

We headed up the stairs hand in hand, in silence. Halfway up the stairs, my urge for him peaked, and I pounced on him, pushing him back against the railing and kissing him again. I pawed at his chest, reaching up and pulling off his jacket. It landed on the stair. He turned to me and pushed me against the railing, kissing me deeply. I reached for the hem of his shirt, pulling it out of his pants and helping him get it over his head until another garment landed on the staircase. The sight of his bare muscled chest excited me even more. I wanted him desperately. The where didn't matter. We heard one of the staff downstairs.

"Not here," he said with a low growl. He grinned mischievously and took my hand. We ran up the stairs together to the bedroom. He closed the door behind me, grabbed me, and lifted me, pressing my back against the door. I wrapped my legs around him, kissing him and running my hands down his back. "Is this what you want?" He asked between breaths and kisses. I dug my fingers into his back.

"And more, lots more," I whispered in his ear.

Second Thoughts

Mornings can be disorienting when traveling or when finding yourself with a new bed partner. When I looked at the handsome and completely naked man asleep next to me, I began to wonder what I was doing. What was I thinking about entertaining him like that? Then again, it had been precisely what I needed. It'd seemed like exactly what he needed as well. I smiled to myself at the memory. It had been a night of incredible passion and satisfaction.

He stirred slightly. His face looked calm as he slept. I could almost see the boy again, or was it a young man? Some memories seemed clear, others just out of reach. I slid out of bed and wrapped myself in a silk robe. I was sitting in the window when there was a tap on the door. It was Roland with a cart of morning juices, fruit, and other interesting-looking finger food. Lazlo sat up in response to the entry. Roland failed to hide the wide grin on his face at the sight of his boss in my bed, although since he also had Lazlo's shirt and jacket on the cart, it was a safe bet he was hardly surprised.

"Should I bring more up for you, Sir?" the two of them were failing to hide the coy smiles I could see passing between them.

"No thanks, Roland, we'll be down shortly," Lazlo said.

Roland nodded and exited the room, closing the door behind him.

"Good morning," my charming bed partner announced as he looked at me. He leaned back as if he was taking in the moment, beaming with pride at his conquest.

I sat where I was, not moving toward him. "Good morning. You look mighty proud of yourself."

He shrugged. "Should I not be? You seemed pleased last night. Is there something you aren't telling me? Something I missed?" He inquired with a hint of pride in his voice. He was clearly in a good mood. Then again, why shouldn't he be?

"Well, based on that exchange I just witnessed between you and Roland, I'm wondering just how batty you've been to your staff recently. How long has it been since *you* acted on that impulse?" I couldn't resist throwing the question he asked me my first day here back at him, not that I was expecting any more of an answer than I gave him.

His look switched to one of slight confusion. "batty?"

I laughed. "You know, crazy or annoying. Batty. Or I could have said bat shit crazy, but apparently, that would have been an even more confusing reference."

He chuckled. "I'm still trying to figure out what bats have to do with anything."

"I suppose they don't. It's a silly expression now that I think about it."

He pointed to my guitar. "And what is that?" he asked.

"My baby," I said.

Lazlo's look of confusion was adorable.

"It's a musical instrument. It's precious to me, so I call it my baby. Don't look so bewildered."

"Do you play?" He asked.

"No, I just like carrying it around with me. Of course, I play."

"So play something for me. Or just leave it and come back to bed," he said, motioning for me to join him.

We locked eyes. I was in no mood to make it easy for him. I grabbed the guitar and pulled it out of the case.

Lazlo contorted his face a bit. "Ouch."

I grinned at him. "No offense, you just win far too easily."

He ran his fingers through his hair. "Apparently not with you."

I shrugged. "You won plenty last night,"

Looking at him sitting there I admired his muscular form, wavy hair, and perfect smile. I felt a wave of longing rip through me again. I gripped the guitar. He wasn't going to get what he wanted that easily.

"I would ask you what you wanted to hear, but I realize it's unlikely we know any of the same songs."

He nodded. "True enough, I've seen and heard much, but my knowledge is limited outside of Vernaria."

I checked the tuning on the instrument and was pleasantly surprised that she'd held her tune well even through this strange journey. She was an electric guitar, so I wasn't sure what this would sound like with no available electricity or amplifier, but Lazlo wouldn't know the difference.

After clicking a few notes, I was amazed at how good the guitar sounded. There was far more life in it without the usual electricity and amplification than expected. I launched into a guitar solo that was a personal favorite of mine. It wasn't quite as brilliant without the electric guitar's full effect, but it sounded pretty decent even with what I had.

As I finished the solo, I looked up. Lazlo was transfixed, staring at me as if he was seeing an alien or some wondrous creature.

"Marjorie," his voice was dark, deep, and sultry.

"Yes." I was curious as to his response.

"I need you, right here, right now," he beckoned me over to the bed.

"You don't want to hear another?" I teased.

"Yes, but later. Right now, get over here, or I'm coming to get you."

"But I want to know what you thought," I said, continuing my ruse of innocence.

"And I want to show you, so put that down and get over here. Or else." he started to slide out of bed.

I slipped out from behind the guitar and put it away as if I was obeying. He was still seated on the bed, but his feet were on the floor, the sheet barely covering anything.

"Or else what?" I asked.

I stood opposite him defiantly, determined to be mischievous. I barely was able to register him standing before Lazlo snatched me in his arms. A slight squeal escaped my lips at my surprise.

He squeezed me tightly and whispered. "You don't get to be so beautiful and so delightful and not in my arms."

"So, you liked it?"

"You," he kissed my neck. "are," the next kiss was on my chest, "amazing," with that, he parted my robe and threw it to the ground as he continued kissing down my body. My knees were going weak. He lifted me and carried me back to the bed, laying me on my back and continuing his kiss onslaught. My skin felt so alive with every touch of his lips. My appetite for him felt endless. I'd never known someone who excited me like this. His kisses were driving me wild. He buried his face in between my legs, demonstrating a skill he'd skipped the night before. I cried out in ecstasy as my body peaked. My body felt limp as he kissed my stomach, working his way up until his face was over mine. He kissed me deeply. I wrapped my legs around him, inviting him into me. As our bodies intertwined, I was lost in the smell and feel of him. Once our mutual desires were satisfied, he collapsed beside me, turning to look at me.

"So," he said still breathing heavily, "are you convinced I enjoyed your playing?"

"Hmm, fairly convinced," I said running a finger down his arm.

"Only fairly?"

"Okay, yeah, that was pretty convincing," I said, "You win."

He reached over and stroked my hair. "It certainly felt like a win."

I looked into his eyes. "Stop it."

He looked confused. "Stop what?"

"Being so damn sexy," I said.

He smiled and kissed me. "I have no intention of discontinuing any behavior that wins me your affection." He sat up and started to slide out of bed. "However, I'd best be getting myself together to start the day," he said, pulling on his pants and taking his shirt and jacket off the cart.

I watched him dress, again admiring his physique. There had been a familiarity in his touch. What all *had* I forgotten?

"Lazlo, did we ever, I mean, before this? Was that why you wanted to marry me? Because you thought you were supposed to?"

He sat on the bed beside me. "Are you remembering something?"

"No, just figuring things out. I know my first time was at

fifteen. Knowing that. . .all I remember about that time was fumbling in the dark. The memory is a bit foggy. It was a boy at school, I liked him a lot. His name was Lance. But it wasn't, was it? It was you."

He wrapped his arm around me. "So what happened to Lance? In your memory?"

"We moved away. I never saw him again. I remember being upset we were leaving, then Gran consoling me and eventually feeling better."

He nodded. "I'd like to think the fumbling in the dark part wasn't accurate but then again, perhaps it was. But yes, by your description Lance is likely what you remember about me."

"I remember he was cute."

Lazlo kissed my head. "I'll take that."

It was interesting, the way my memory had been manipulated. Things changed just enough so that they'd line up with what was true. But why we left, even in that memory, why we moved, I could find nothing other than because Gran said so.

I placed a hand on his thigh. " I wish I could remember."

"Well, I think you're perfect either way," he said leaning his head to touch mine. "But, if you don't mind . . ."

"Yes, starting your day, I know. It's fine."

He kissed me again. "Then, I'll see you downstairs shortly."

He turned and walked out of the room, leaving me alone with my thoughts.

******

By the time I'd dressed and joined him in the dining room, he was laughing and having a pleasant moment with the carriage driver. Suddenly I realized I was clueless about the driver's name. I hadn't even seen him since my first night here.

Lazlo stood up straighter when he noticed me walking into

the room. His eyes sparkled, and he smiled like a child about to open a present.

"Good morning, again," he said with that smile still broad across his face.

God, he's so damn sexy. My eyes shifted to the driver.

"I don't believe I was ever properly introduced," I said.

"Of course, my apologies," Lazlo began, but before he could say more, the driver spoke for himself.

"The name is Arthur, and you, of course, are the legendary Marjorie. Indeed it is a pleasure to meet one I've heard so much talk about," he said, shifting his eyes to Lazlo.

As color rushed to my cheeks at that, I realized that I wasn't the only one slightly embarrassed when looking at Lazlo. He recovered quickly, looking at me and shrugging.

As we convened over breakfast, I decided now was as good a time as any to bring up my need to leave. "Lazlo, to create the barrier that will allow you to leave to go find your mother, I need a few things."

"Of course, name it, make a list, and we'll have it delivered, or I'll get it when I'm in town."

"Actually, that won't work. I need to leave for a bit on my own. I need to find your sister."

Lazlo looked deep in thought, furrowed brows, and brought his arms across his chest. "You knew this last night. You didn't tell me. You had plenty of opportunity. Plenty. More than plenty," he said.

He leveled his eyes at me. He was not at all happy. Perhaps by his look, he felt a bit betrayed.

"I'm sorry. I planned on it when I asked you to meet with me, but, well, it went differently than I'd planned," I said.

His eyes were fixed on me, unmoving. He looked pissed.

"Differently? Don't play games with me, Marjorie. You were the one who asked to see me. You were the one who wanted more. That isn't on me; that was your idea. At any moment, you could have had this discussion with me."

His stare was intimidating. This hadn't been at all what I wanted. I knew he wouldn't be thrilled at the idea, to begin with, but I hadn't expected such a strong response.

Unexpected emotions flooded me. "I'm not. I don't mean to." My lip trembled, my eyes were starting to water. It wasn't a game; I didn't want to hurt him. I felt terrible, but why the hell was I tearing up? Why did he affect me like this?

"Shit," Lazlo said as he uncrossed his arms and shifted back into his chair. "Fine. Don't get upset. I'll support you in this, alright. I just wasn't expecting it after last night. I thought . . .well, I trusted you were being honest with me."

I closed my eyes to recompose myself and nodded. "I was honest with you. I just neglected to share that information."

"An interesting way of putting it," he said.

"I'm sorry I didn't say anything." I had to look away from him. "I need you to tell me where I can find Gwen, or have the best chance of finding her. This is a critical piece, and everything points to it being something she has, or if she doesn't have it, knows where it should be."

"I know where she is. I can give you that information," he said. His tone was flat. "Might I inquire how long before you need to embark on this journey?" he asked.

"Perhaps as soon as later today or possibly starting fresh tomorrow morning. It depends on how far away Gwen is."

"It's a day's journey by train. Not close, but not that far," he said.

"Thank you. There was mention of another library I haven't

found yet, a blue room? Can you show me?" I asked.

Lazlo nodded and stood. "Come now, and I'll show you." It wasn't only his tone; his body language toward me had shifted. He'd expected better of me, more honesty from me, and I'd disappointed him.

As we walked into this unique library, I turned to the massive bookshelves, all in different shapes and all in blue. Lazlo made sure I knew how the library was organized before taking his leave to see to his duties.

One book in particular I suspected would hold the key to what I needed. I went to work finding it, along with a few more that contained additional information I thought would be useful. Thoughts of Lazlo crept in. I hated that I'd disappointed him. I shoved the thoughts aside, determined to focus on the work at hand.

After several hours of complete immersion, I realized I was hungry. As if by magic or mind-reading, Lazlo suddenly appeared at the entrance of the blue room.

"It's getting rather late. Are you staying here tonight, and would you like to join me for dinner, or are you rushing off soon?" he asked.

"I'll leave in the morning. Now that you mention it, I'm famished," I confessed.

He extended his arm. "Then walk with me, or would you prefer to change first?"

I put aside my books and strolled across the room.

"Is it alright with you if I skip that tonight?" I asked, taking his arm.

"Quite alright, if that's your pleasure," he said, leading me down the hall.

"You know, Marjorie, I'm beginning to learn more about our

differences,

Still, after giving it more thought, I think we could do very well as a team."

I nodded. "I understand your views. But just please lay off the relationship pressure. As much as I like you, it freaks me out."

I regretted those words instantly. Was I playing games? It wasn't my intention.

Lazlo gave me a confused look. "Freaks you out?"

"Sorry, it, well, makes me uncomfortable."

"Well, in that case, I apologize if you have felt pressured or uncomfortable. It was never my intention."

"I didn't feel pressured last night," I said as I looked up at him.

"I should think not, since, after all, it was your idea, not that I didn't agree wholeheartedly," Lazlo said with a smile.

His expression lifted my spirits. He didn't look upset at my previous comment. For my part, the mere reminder of our heated time together was thrilling. There was no doubt in my mind that if I could take him as a lover without worrying about commitment, I'd be signing on pronto. The arranged marriage part, or the marriage part in general, frightened me. I couldn't wrap my head around him wanting that.

As we neared the dining room, I could smell freshly baked bread and other delectable smells coming from the kitchen. I immediately remembered my hunger. Lazlo ushered me in and pulled out a chair to seat me. Wealthy, handsome, well-mannered, a virtual sex god and adored me; even I struggled a bit to understand my reluctance to claim what would be a fantastic prize to most women.

Our dinner conversation was light and devoid of any frightening subjects. He stayed after dinner a while, and we continued chatting. I was thankful for the extra time with him. Still, his expression from this morning haunted me. I didn't like disappointing him. That was a sign my attraction was more than physical. I cared what he thought. He mattered to me. I brushed that thought aside.

Enchantment

Lazlo led me to my bedroom, kissed me gently, and bid me a good sleep. No one had refused anyone. He was merely giving me the space I'd requested. Space I wasn't sure I wanted but thought I needed. Still, I was a bit upset he hadn't even tried. He made no move whatsoever.

The distance I wanted to remedy was back. It was my fault. I'd taken him to my bed. There was an unspoken expectation that came with that exchange of passion. It included a level of honesty that I didn't live up to. Still, he could've tried. If he truly wanted me, that is.

The more I thought about it, the more it irritated me. Last night and this morning, he was all over me. Then he just leaves me in my bedroom and walks away. I changed into my nightdress and sat on the edge of the bed. I ran the scenario over and over again in my head. Why didn't he protest at least a little? Was he that fragile? He certainly didn't seem that way.

There was a light knock at the door. The voice from the hallway was Roland bringing in some late-night refreshments.

I realized I had no idea exactly where Lazlo's room was in the large manor and felt a burning urge to talk to him and give him my opinions on his behavior.

"Roland,"

"Yes, M'Lady," he said politely.

"Would you tell Lazlo I need to speak with him?"

"I will pass that on when he returns. It may be late, however," Roland said.

Returns? My mind immediately began racing. Where the hell did he go? Is that why he abandoned me to go hook up with some other chick? Was he looking for other marriage prospects? I felt ill to my stomach.

"Where did he go, may I ask?" I responded with every ounce of calm I could muster.

"He is training M'Lady. He does this every evening typically. He is on the grounds, but I'm not allowed to know exactly where or to interrupt, even if I were to come across him."

That calmed me down a bit and kind of explained all of those muscles. A physique like his would require maintenance.

"Would you still like me to relay your request when he returns?" Roland asked.

Now I had a decision to make, unobstructed by heated emotion. If I said yes, then Lazlo might come in while I was asleep. If I said no, then Lazlo might never know I'd had this meltdown. I stood there, thinking while Roland waited patiently. I then realized that saying no wasn't going to spare me his knowledge of my having asked. Roland was still likely to tell him I'd been asking after him. Then he might show up anyway, but that would be his idea, not mine. I wanted as much to be on my terms as possible.

"Yes, Roland. Please tell him I'd like to see him."

There I did it. I said it. I asked for him. Then I started to worry. What if he didn't come? What if he was mad at me or didn't want me if I wasn't willing to commit? My mind was too full of possibilities. It was making me crazy.

I did what I usually do when I'm feeling anxious. I got out my guitar and started playing. There was a comfort to simply holding it in my hands. The weight of the instrument, its smooth body, the strings digging into my fingers soothed me. When I'd played it for Lazlo before, it'd sounded decent, as if something may have been flowing through it. I wondered about this place. I wondered about what might work. I began to tune into the energies surrounding me. Magic works so much better here; it's so unobstructed.

Power lit up my fingertips as I focused. The guitar responded as if it was alive and full of electricity with its own amplification. Magic and music together! It was heaven. I began playing and singing song after song. It was effortless. I was alive with energy, lost in the sounds of my guitar, my voice.

I was rocking out a tune when I noticed him standing in the doorway, leaning against the door frame, smiling. His hair looked damp with sweat. I stopped as soon as I saw him, somewhat startled by what seemed to be his sudden appearance.

"You asked for me. Here I am. Don't stop on my account, however," he said.

The magic was still coursing through me. It felt exhilarating.

"This is amazing! My guitar shouldn't be working like this, but it is. I can feel the magic flowing through me into my instrument and then out again," I said.

"I must say I've never heard sounds like that before, nor seen anyone channel magic like that. The ancestors on this side are all buzzing, doing their best to assemble as close as allowed to your phenomenon. I've never seen anything like it. You continue to amaze me, Marjorie. Is this why you asked me here to show me this? I'm surprised Roland would fail to mention something so spectacular."

Now I was embarrassed. I'd asked him here to soothe a wounded ego. He'd fully respected my wishes, and I'd had mixed feelings about him doing so. Now seeing him standing there, feeling as wonderful as I did with the magic coursing through me, it seemed silly.

"I didn't discover this until after Roland left. I apologize. I didn't mean to interrupt your evening routine. I confess I regretted asking you to leave me alone tonight. You walked away, and I wished you hadn't. That was why I asked for you," I said.

That was as plain as I wanted to be, and it was truthful without confessing to any near meltdown.

"And then you found something to bring you joy. I'm glad you asked me here. I wouldn't have wanted to miss this, both the wonderful performance and your glee. I love seeing you happy," he said.

I noticed he still hadn't come into the room. He was remaining respectful of the boundaries I'd set even though I'd confessed I wanted him here.

"Do you want me to stay here with you tonight? I will if you ask it of me. It would certainly be my pleasure. All I ask is that you are honest with me about what you want," he said.

Smooth and sexy, and either not mad at me or setting it aside.

"Only if that doesn't upset your normal routine. I feel I've challenged you enough for now."

He laughed. "Challenged certainly. That seems a fitting description for you. Still, I'm happy to stay here with you." Lazlo entered the room and sat on the bed. "I'm your captive audience. Play as long as you like or come to bed. I'm here for you either way."

There were plenty of things I was still dying to play, and sometimes music is a way to express a feeling, when regular words don't come, so I took the opportunity he presented.

"Just one more, if that's alright. For you."

He nodded. "Of course."

I pooled the energies in and allowed them to flow, giving life to my instrument as I channeled a tune I'd been working on, one I'd written myself. I sang at the top of my lungs, belting out the song with all the passion in my heart. It had never sounded this beautiful, this magical. Light glistened off my fingers. It felt as if I was casting a spell.

If Lazlo had looked surprised the first time I played for him, he looked utterly overwhelmed this time. I had hit a button. No, I had hit a home run. He was captivated. I'd enchanted a powerful mage.

I put away the guitar and crossed to him. I straddled his legs, my arms around his neck, and pulled his head into my chest. His large hands slipped up my back, and we began to melt together as he covered me with kisses. He slipped me out of my nightdress, lifted me into his arms, and put me on the bed. I watched him as he undressed, his eyes never leaving me. He climbed onto the bed. I reached for him, wrapping my arms around him. His broad body surrounded me as we merged into each other. While the night before had been our hunger, our need, this night, our connection felt magical. I had cast a spell that was not only holding him but drawing me in as well. I'd never felt so loved in all my life.

******

Neither of us had awoken before Roland knocked on the door with my morning tray. Lazlo was the one to respond.

"Come on in, Roland."

Roland grinned, apparently happy Lazlo was still here.

He scooted the cart in and turned to Lazlo. "Will the two of you be having breakfast downstairs, or should I bring more up for you?"

"We'll be down, Roland. Marjorie has a train to catch. We won't be long."

"Very good, Sir. I will see you both downstairs." Roland offered a polite bow at the waist before heading on his way.

Lazlo turned to me. "As much as I don't want to see you leave, I won't stand in the way of you catching the train you need. I hope when you return, we can have more relaxing mornings together," he said as he traced my face with his finger and looked into my eyes.

I found myself wanting to stay. I didn't want to be without him. Still, if we were to take the next logical step in unlocking some of these mysteries, I needed Gwen's information. It was clear there were no telephones here, so I had to make the trip instead.

"Lazlo," my hand went to his chest. "I'm so glad you're here with me right now. I don't want to leave you. I never meant to say anything to hurt you," I said.

He smiled. "I will always come when you ask me, and your apology is accepted."

"I guess I need to gather some things to get ready," I said.

I'd done very little to prepare for this trip. As I jumped up to look around at what I might need, Lazlo was getting out of bed and beginning to get dressed. I proceeded to scan my clothes to do the same.

"I want to grab a few things before you leave. I won't be long. I'll see you in the dining room," Lazlo said as he pulled on his shirt.

I nodded. He tipped my chin up to kiss me goodbye before he walked out the door. What happened last night with the music was still on my mind, as was what happened with Lazlo. It was as if I'd discovered a new form of magic within myself, a magic that worked through music. As for Lazlo, our connection was growing. He was letting himself be vulnerable with me, and I was feeling far more vulnerable with him than I had planned or thought possible.

With this spinning in my head, I gathered a few items in a bag to take with me. I didn't think I would need much. Gwen was only a day's journey away.

******

When I arrived downstairs, Lazlo was speaking with Arthur and Roland. It appeared he was giving them some direction.

"Good morning, again." He smiled as I walked in.

He hadn't bothered to change from the attire he had worn last night, but his face was radiant. I smiled, feeling like I was a girl again with a crush on some boy at school.

"There's a favor I want to ask you before you leave," Lazlo said.

"What do you need?" I asked.

"I want to offer you extra protection, an exchange of energies that will allow us to signal each other if needed. Would you be willing to do that?"

"Um, I'm certain you and I have exchanged plenty of energy by now," I said. Damnit, why did I always bring it back to the sex?

He chuckled. "Nothing that complicated or enjoyable, just give me your hand." In his hand was a clear blue crystal. When I put my hand in his, it began to radiate heat, and hues of green, purple and blue were radiating out from it between our palms. Suddenly I felt it snap, and the light and heat subsided. Lazlo withdrew his hand, and I could see two crystals now, both dark in color instead of the clear blue one from before. Lazlo picked up a chain from on the table. The crystal itself slid easily onto it. He stood up and placed it around my neck.

"I'll be wearing the other half. You can use this to reach me if you need me, and I can also signal you if new information comes my way that you may need."

"Thanks, I'm sure I'll be fine, but I appreciate it."

"It'll make me feel better, stuck here while you do work that I ought to be doing. Thank you, for aiding me in this. It's been frustrating being unable to bring that errant spirit back and stop whatever damage it may be doing while wearing my mother's form."

"What exactly has it been doing? Do you hear rumors?"

"It's difficult to know what in particular is related to her, and every time I hear of a magical atrocity, I worry. Mother may not be wholly innocent in this either," Lazlo said

"How so? I mean, she is possessed, isn't' she?" I asked.

"She wasn't happy here even though this is her ancestral home. My strong-willed mother may or may not aid us in removing that possession depending on her desires. That's my fear," he said.

"Lazlo." I paused, unsure of what to say. He looked at me expectantly, intrigued by the long pause but keeping silent as if to honor it.

"I... well, what I want to say is thank you. In this brief time, you've shown me and shared so much with me. I'm unsure what lies ahead, but I do look forward to knowing more about you, knowing you, who you've become, much better," I said.

He smiled gently with a reassuring look. "I too look forward to that. However, as much as I would love to continue this conversation, I believe you have a train to catch. Roland has already loaded your luggage, and Arthur is ready to take you to the station. Oh, and Beatrice insisted on a basket of goodies for your trip as well," he said as he handed me the basket.

He escorted me to the door. As I turned to walk out, he grabbed my arm and pulled me in close to him. Our faces were nose to nose. He pushed a strand of my hair out of my face, still looking at me. The electricity between us felt as if it was pulling our faces closer, our lips met, and he kissed me as passionately as he had the night before. He pulled away, allowing me some space before whispering, "Come back to me, Marjorie".

I nodded, realizing at that moment there was some fear on his part that I was going to disappear on him again. I wanted to turn to him and tell him how much I adored him. Instead, I turned out the door and stepped into the carriage. This time I could see the road. There was no fog, the morning was clear, and the view was stunning.

Danger Abroad

When I boarded the train, it was clear this was a busy place. There had been a few people at the station, but plenty more were on board. Travel by train seemed a normal mode of transportation in this realm. A few looks shifted my way as my attire wasn't quite the norm. The clothes Lazlo had brought in looked far too aristocratic, so I'd chosen from my own limited wardrobe. It was somewhat eccentric, but it wasn't scandalous. I made my way to an empty seat and pulled out my book. A young woman with bright blue eyes and luxurious blonde hair spoke to me.

"Mind if I join you?" she asked.

I shrugged. "Not at all," I said, despite my desire to be left alone.

"I'm Mary," she said as she took the seat across from me.

"Nice to meet you, Mary. I'm Marjorie."

As we moved onward, Mary prattled on about how she was traveling to see her brother, who was supposed to get her into this prestigious school that no one in their family had gotten into, but he had this friend and on and on. Although I desperately wanted to do my work, I feigned interest and nodded periodically.

My mind wandered to Lazlo. What was I doing with him?

He'd made it clear he needed to marry, and much as I was beginning to like him, that idea still frightened me. I wasn't sure I could let that person be me.

Suddenly movement on Mary's bag caught my attention. A small creature was crawling out. It was shimmering blue, with wings that were glistening in the sunlight streaming through the window. There was a playful look in its eyes as it looked directly at me and grinned. Or at least I think it was a grin. It began to float up above Mary. Mary began to wind down her story and started to turn toward the creature. Sensing it didn't want to be seen by her, I decided to interact with her more directly.

"Mary, can I ask you something?" I managed to get a question in without grossly interrupting her flow. Her endless chatter had already informed me she was a single woman with a strong interest in men.

"Of course you can!" She said, eager for conversation.

"It's about men," I said.

Her eyes widened "oooh, of course." She grinned, and I got the sense I was about to be given plenty of advice.

"First thing I'd say, sweetie, is that outfit isn't doing you any favors. I mean, you need something more figure-flattering if you really want to get his attention. Nothing wrong with the way you dress. I'm only suggesting such an interesting-looking woman such as yourself could highlight herself better."

Interesting looking? That was a first. I'd been called a lot of things but not that. I smiled.

"Thanks for that insight, but that isn't the problem. He wants me to marry him, and I barely know him. At least not as an adult. See, we knew each other when we were younger, then recently reconnected, and I don't feel I truly know him or that he can truly know me. Not who we've become now as adults. I fear he wants his memory of me and not so much the real woman in front of him." There, I said it. My most troubling concern floating out there as I told it to a complete stranger. What if he loved who I was and not who I am?

The somewhat blank look on her face told me she'd not been expecting that type of question. She reached out and put her hand on top of mine.

"Oh my, I feel as if I've just read the most amazing romance story just by hearing your words. A man in love with you from childhood? Ah, how blissfully romantic? But how has he changed? Is he not appealing, not what you want? There must be something holding you back other than what you expressed. Did he grow up unattractive?"

"This will sound crazy," I said. Suddenly I felt fully engaged in girl talk and realized how much I needed this at the moment. "But he's everything I've ever dreamed of, handsome, strong, kind, easy to be around. I adore him. But I also treasure my freedom."

She cocked her head, evaluating me at the moment. "What freedom do you want? The freedom to be alone forever, to never have a sense of security? Admittedly having no responsibility to anyone is rather freeing, but at the same time, isn't it lonely?" She paused, gauging my response. I sat there, looking confused. There was so much going through my mind.

These past few weeks since losing Gran had been the only time in my life I'd been truly alone. Her words were giving me plenty to consider.

"Or is his style rather authoritarian so that you don't think you'd ever have a chance to breathe? I tend not to invite those men even to have a chance. The suitors I mentioned in my life all are men who, at least on the surface, aren't going to chain me to the house, but the two of us will have a partnership and have a glorious life together, possibly raising a family. That's what I'm seeking. Doesn't that appeal to you?" The little creature was making faces from its perch. It was adorable. I couldn't help but smile.

Still, despite its amusing distraction, I had to admit Mary had a point. I'd always thought of being married and having a family as giving up on my dreams. The view of it as a partnership opened an idea I hadn't allowed myself to consider yet. Gran had always been there for me, made me feel as if I had a life partner. The thought of being without Lazlo was unappealing. As loathe as I felt to admit it, in this short time, he'd become important to me.

"Thank you, when you put it that way, it gives me a new perspective," I said.

We felt the train slowing down, and the attendant announced the next stop.

"This is me. Well, it's been lovely chatting! Take care, Marjorie, and don't let that man get away. He does sound like a keeper," Mary said as she grabbed her immediate belongings and left the car.

The train started up again and there was no more chattering. My mind wandered. I started imagining what it might be like to switch my plans and settle down instead of embracing the wandering gypsy life I'd planned. With Lazlo, I'd not have to worry; so long as we had a child, the book would not be lost. Still, I was determined to break that curse because even if I had children, I didn't want to burden them the way I felt burdened.

My hand went to the crystal around my neck. Lazlo's energy gently pulsated through it at my touch. It was nice to have this connection. This time away gave me a chance to reflect. What did I feel when I thought of him? He was amazing, more incredible than any man I'd ever known. But marriage? Maybe if we sorted out his family issues, the two of us could date. I could still travel on my own, sometimes with him. That sounded like something I could get behind.

Suddenly I sensed something at my feet. A small furry animal that looked a bit like a fox was underneath my seat. The blue flying creature was still perched above the window. The energy of both creatures was comforting, soothing. The train droned on. I stared out the window, watching the countryside go by. Before long, my tired eyes closed and drifted into sleep.

******

The train suddenly lurching to a stop. A woman screamed. Before I was fully aware of what was happening, a large hand wrapped around my arm. Startled and still half asleep, I resisted little when the man pulled me into the aisle of the train car. The necklace with the crystal was abruptly ripped off of my neck and tossed aside. Several men grabbed bags and pulled other passengers off the train, throwing their luggage and other belongings into a pile.

A large man pushed me against the train wall, sniffing my hair and pawing at me. One hand groped at my breasts while the other was at the hem of my skirt, lifting it. My mind was racing. I instinctively tried to summon my forces to push him away, nothing happened. I uttered a silent incantation, still nothing. My magic wasn't working. With no other options available, I kicked him, not hitting any decent target, but hard enough to annoy him. I'd never been much good as a fighter.

"Well, what do you know, a fighter. Hey, guys, throw me the rope. This one wants to kick."

The men were quick to obey his request. He threw me to the floor, and while securing my hands and feet, growled in my ear. "You and me are gonna have some fuuuuuun later."

I felt sick, desperate to get away but powerless. He began to carry me to their awaiting buggy. Determined to make it difficult for him, I squirmed and kicked as violently as possible. He dropped me as we headed down the stairs off the train. I screamed from the pain of the landing. I scrambled as best as I could with my restraints, but there was nowhere to go. He quickly and easily lifted me again before throwing me into the gang's waiting carriage.

I was stacked on top of some of the travelers' belongings and saw no other people. Apparently, I was the only person of interest to these men; a terrifying thought. I did my best to keep my calm. Spending energy on freaking out wasn't going to help me escape. I hadn't seen an option yet, but there had to be one.

It wasn't long until several men were inside the carriage with the rest on the outside, and the vehicle was in motion. Why no magic was working, I didn't understand. This place, this realm, was full of it. But my access was blocked.

The carriage stopped, and when they pulled me out, we were at a cabin in a wooded area. Once inside, I continued my struggles while three of them secured me to a small cot in the back of the cabin. One of the men had a touch that felt like fire. When his skin hit mine, a jolt of pain went through my body. I'd never experienced anything like it before. It was agonizing. I wasn't left there long before the one with the painful touch returned with the man who had grabbed me on the train. "I tied her up good, boss, just like you said."

"Good job, Togy. You'll do your part later, but since she can't do much right now, I think I'd like to enjoy her for a while to get this party off to a proper start."

The smelly man crawled on top of me. "Where do I begin, witch whore? Oh, you thought I didn't know, did you? I can smell the magic on you. That's why you're here, in fact. But not doing you much good now, is it? You magic types fuck over the rest of us; it's only fair we get turn around. I'm gonna enjoy every second of this."

His hand went up my skirt, grabbed my panties, and tore them off.

I shook my head. "No," I squeaked.

"It doesn't matter. Suit yourself." He crawled on top of me and began to penetrate me. I closed my eyes, desperate to be anywhere other than here. He growled and grumbled; his hot, smelly breath was nearly choking me as I tried again to distance myself from my body. At length he finished, and moved away. My body was shaking, tears rolling down my face.

"She's a good one. I think she'll fetch a pretty penny," he announced as he put himself back together.

Once I was no longer the center of attention, the men turned to discuss their plans. I had thought I was an unfortunate victim of chance that spared any other females on the train from this treatment, but as I pretended to be passed out, I heard a different discussion that alarmed me even more.

"I think we secured us the big money prize this time. Togy, you have proven your worth. That witch whore, they are willing to pay top dollar for a bitch like that. She was helpless and easy to catch, thanks to you. She can't do any magic right now, but I can smell it on her. She's strong, that one. The buyers will be here tomorrow to evaluate the prize we collected for them. We'll know just how large our profits are once they decide what the bitch is worth."

"To Togy!" The men raised glasses and began to drink. It seemed that somehow Togy rendered my magic useless. I'd learned some magical defensive skills with Gran. They were usually all I needed if I got into a bad situation, but this was terrifying. Plus, I'd never heard of someone smelling magic, but this leader had such an ability.

While they weren't paying attention, I examined my prospects. The crystal attaching me to Lazlo, the one I was supposed to use to communicate with him, was gone. I couldn't see it in any of the piles of things they had gathered. The ropes tying my arms and legs were secure. I wasn't the first bound victim, of that I was sure.

Pretending to be asleep didn't stop a drunken man from coming over and pawing at me, groping my breasts as I could see through half-closed eyes, him readying himself to continue my humiliation. I pretended to stir, keeping the ruse going, but he didn't care, moved into position and began his ritual. Once in place, he continued his thrusting. He only said words like "oh yeah," "feels so good," as if I wasn't even there. I was terrified. What was going to happen to me? After overhearing their conversation, I wasn't sure how long I had to live. Was I more valuable alive or dead? Was this to be my fate?

The Warrior

As the sun began to beam through a window, the men were rising. Those that hadn't been fully dressed were dressing. Several were sharing cups of warm tea or coffee while others were chattering about what to do with all the money they would get from this heist.

"Alright, Togy, your chance to shine. Neutralize this bitch before they get here so she won't give them any trouble."

Togy eagerly whipped out his manhood and pounced on top of me. While the others had been humiliating, his mere touch was painful. This was excruciating. I became desperate to escape, thrashing against my bonds. Togy's hands landed on my shoulders, lighting my skin on fire, pinning me down even more firmly as I moved my legs as much as the ropes would allow trying to get him off of me. It was as if every cell in my body was rejecting him, like this was an abomination.

My body was screaming from the inside out. I couldn't stop it. I was in full panic mode. A sound escaped my body, a sound I'd never heard myself make before. It felt as if it shattered something far above us. "Oh, she's a strong one, boss, I can feel it, oh . . ." When he released into me, I felt sick, a sickness like I've never felt before. My head was spinning, my entire body weak. I turned my head and vomited.

After he moved away, the boss came over and sat me up, half-heartedly straightening my clothes. "Gotta make you look more presentable for our buyers, witch."

My tears started falling again out of terror, out of pain.

"Oh, don't cry. I'm sure they'll keep you well entertained. I hear those guys love to fuck witches too, the ones they don't grind up, that is," he said.

He signaled for one of the men to take me to another part of the cabin. Walking was painful. Everything hurt inside me. When he sat me down again, my sobbing intensified; my insides were in such pain. I wondered what Lazlo was doing. I wished I'd just stayed with him. I wondered how he could ever want me now, even if I did survive. I vomited on the floor.

There was a sudden bang as the door of the cabin flew open. The men jumped back. Filling the doorway was a large man, sword drawn. My head was still spinning. My eyes couldn't focus. Was it Lazlo? The men fumbled, looking for their weapons. The warrior moved straight for Togy, sword in hand. Togy stood there, unmoving, staring. With one swift blow, Togy's head was severed. Both body and head fell lifeless to the floor with the blood splatter decorating the nearby furniture.

The gang leader sprinted toward me. A knife flew from the warrior's hand and buried itself deep in the back of his neck. He slumped to the floor. Two of the men ran for the door. The warrior swiftly cut them down in two sharp, brutal swings. The last two men in the cabin charged him. With incredible speed, he sliced through both of them. They never stood a chance. Their bodies fell to the floor. I sat there stunned, still unsure of what I saw while the warrior checked the bodies for life. Once he seemed satisfied that the danger had been nullified, he rushed to my side. I wasn't dreaming. It was him, it was Lazlo.

I was thrilled to see him and horrified to have him see me like this. The little fox and blue flying creature were in the doorway, neither wanting to come inside to the terrible scene. Lazlo crouched beside me.

"Marjorie, are you alright? No, of course, you aren't. How idiotic of me to ask. This is terrible. I should never have allowed you to go on your own. Can you ever forgive me?"

I looked at him, somewhat bewildered. "How did, I mean, where… what? Thank you," was all I could manage. I reached for him, wrapped my arms around him, and buried my head on his chest.

"Your little friends over there are who you have to thank. They took the crystal and found me and led me back to you." He handed me a leather wineskin. "Here, drink this; it tastes terrible, but it'll help you regain some strength. We need to be clear of here before their constituents arrive. Can you walk?"

Dutifully I drank some of the liquid he handed me. It was difficult to choke down, but I managed. The shame of what I'd just been through began flooding through me, but it was nothing compared to the illness I was feeling in my body. I knew my legs were shaky, but suddenly I realized I didn't want him to see me as weak or helpless or worry him any more than he already was.

"I can walk," I said, and with that, summoning all the remaining strength in my body, I stood up.

"Good, then let's get you out of here and somewhere safe. I'll stay and defend you if necessary, but we're better off if we can move. If you need me to carry you, please don't hesitate to say. I'll manage. Your well-being is my priority. Are any of these things yours?"

"Nothing that I want is here, aside from the book."

The book came to me as I held out my hand. Death must have destroyed whatever ability Togy had to mute magic. I assumed that when I saw Lazlo go for him first. I wondered what it was he had done to me. Was it part of his abilities? I shoved the thought from my mind. At least the book still came to me.

I stepped over the bodies and through the thick, glistening pools of blood everywhere. I felt nothing for these corpses, no sorrow, not even anger, hatred, or resentment. Just nothing.

The pain in my body was growing, but I was managing it. The bitter-tasting liquid Lazlo had shared did help with my footing. I was strong. Nothing could stop me. I was going to live, that much I knew, and that relief was all I needed. My head was still spinning; I felt like throwing up but choked back the impulse.

We walked out of the cabin and into the wooded area secluding it. Leaves crunched beneath our feet. I felt a chill pass through me, although the air itself wasn't cold. The little creatures began chirping, one at our feet and the other circling my head. I couldn't understand exactly, but I knew they were guiding us somewhere. Lazlo seemed aware of it as well. He unhitched the horses from the carriage, pointed them in the opposite direction, and gave each a solid slap so that they went running.

"That should confuse the men they called here. I'll cover our foot tracks as we go. Since the carnage shows no sign of magic, they might suspect the men angered the wrong person, and there wasn't any magic here. I hadn't heard of their hunting in this area, but now that we know, we must exercise extra caution."

I desperately wanted to ask him questions. Who were those men? Why did they want witches as opposed to other women? Did they kidnap male magic users as well? All the things I found myself wondering were mashing together in my head. There was so much I didn't know. Instead of asking, I followed in silence.

Lazlo was walking with his hand ready on the hilt of his sword. He was still on high alert. After the blood bath, he'd cleaned his weapons and retrieved his knife from the neck of the ringleader.

Our interesting friends had fallen silent as we moved through the wooded area, doing our best not to make noise, swishing through the fallen leaves that covered the ground. I could hear words of comfort from them inside my head, in addition to directional senses.

After we'd all walked in silence and were clear of the cabin and surrounding area, Lazlo stopped and turned to me. "Do you need to rest at all? We can stop for a moment if you need it."

That was all he asked, and for that, I was thankful. No questions about my ordeal, no questions about what hurts, just checking in. Perhaps my physical and emotional pain was evident in my demeanor or assumed. Either way, I was grateful not to be quizzed about it.

I shook my head. "No, I'm okay for now," I lied. "Let's keep going, wherever it is that we're going." With every step, I felt the stabbing pains inside me growing stronger.

"Alright," he said softly. There was pain in his eyes. From what he'd said before he felt at least partially responsible for what had happened to me. For my part, as far as my mind was concerned, he had no blame whatsoever. Even if he had detailed warnings, I know I would have ignored them, determined to carve my own path, to do what I thought needed to be done. I still felt I needed to find his sister. I wasn't sure how that might play out at this point, but I knew I needed to connect with her. However, I knew I was in poor shape at the moment. I was not as sharp as I needed to be, especially with what I'd discovered about the dangers present.

He took my hand, still looking as if he was on high alert. The warmth of his hand against mine was comforting. We traveled in silence again, stopping if he heard or saw anything to make sure no one spotted us.

The pain was getting worse. The sun was beginning to drop in the sky, and I knew I was nearing the end of my ability to keep going. I'd pushed aside my feelings, but something was happening in my body. My pulse was racing. I was so hot. Sweat started to pour from my face. My knees buckled and I began to fall. Strong arms caught me, preventing me from landing in the pile of leaves beneath me.

I could barely see; my vision was so blurred. "You are burning up." I heard Lazlo say. "How much further?" he said to the creatures. "She is worse than I thought."

He lifted me into his arms, carrying me through the trees. His pace faster than before, even with my added weight in his arms. I felt myself slipping in and out of consciousness. My body was on fire. I could feel fluid dripping down my leg. Something was horribly wrong.

The White Lady

"Greetings, dear ones." An ethereal-sounding voice filled my head, or was I hearing it? I wasn't sure. Something small, perhaps a woman, glowing white, appeared from behind a tree. The glow was so bright and my vision so blurred I couldn't make out any features. Leaves rustled as our two small magical friends rushed to greet her.

"Thank you, my friends, for bringing her to me," she said as she reached down to pat the top of the little fox's head and gestured at the blue sprite flitting around him.

She stood and faced Lazlo. "Brave one, you cannot come inside, but we thank you for your service."

I felt my body being shifted from Lazlo's arms onto what felt like some type of stretcher. He bowed to her.

"Will you bring her back here? I'm happy to wait if that is needed."

"Yes, we will bring her back to this spot by the time the sun begins to rise again, and you can continue to assist her in her journey."

Lazlo bowed again. "Thank you for your assistance and aid."

She nodded to him as they carried me through to an opening that had appeared. Pain shot through me; it felt as if something was burning me from the inside. I cried out. She held my hand,

and the pain decreased. "Come, my child, we will see to your healing."

A light surrounded us and continued to build. When it died down, I could tell we were no longer in the forest but in a tent. I vomited off of the side of the stretcher, surprised there was anything left in my stomach. A small creature was quickly cleaning it up.

There was another lady with blue hair, and one whose dark purple hair had a few pink strands. The white lady motioned to a bath or pool that I could see just beyond the tent. There was steam rising off of it.

"Disrobe her and get her into the pool. Quickly. We haven't much time. We have plenty of work to do."

My body was on fire, still stiff with pain. I felt as if I was about to shut down entirely. They undressed me and slipped me into the pool. Beautiful smells surrounded me as I sunk into the warm water. It felt as if it was caressing my body gently, holding me so softly and perfectly. Immediately my head began spinning again; the world around me felt as if it was moving at lightning speed.

There was a sense of power, beautiful pure power. I couldn't maintain consciousness, nor did I want to. In that dream-altered state, I saw the white lady moving lights, balls of energy around me, around the room. They entered my body, through my skin, lighting up every cell. I was part of the power itself; pieces were falling away, leaving me. I couldn't move or respond, only feel and sense, and there was no fear or loss of power in this. It felt natural somehow. Part of my brain was amazed that I didn't fear this unusual experience. Deep inside me, I knew this was right. I slipped further under until I could sense no more.

******

When I opened my eyes, the room was full of sunlight. Sitting upright and looking around, I realized I was dressed in new clothes, on a cot, and no longer in the pool. The white lady was entering the tent. She smiled at me.

"How do you feel, dear one?"

At that moment, checking in with my body, I realized the pain was gone. Only a remnant remained, a ghost of the pain. I felt more myself again.

"Much better, thank you."

"The anti-magic would have killed you eventually had we not intervened. Others survive it, but you would not have due to the nature of magic in your lineage."

"My lineage?" I'd never heard anything about what I knew of my family that made our magic any different, so I was curious.

Another woman entered the tent and whispered something to her. She nodded and turned back to me, ignoring my inquiry.

"We removed all of that anti-magic essence, but some things would not let go under our power. There were many dark soul fragments attached to you. Some from this, many are ancestral. You'll have to find the power within yourself to release them fully," she said.

I was still trying to process all of this. The magic in this realm was unlike anything I knew, or at least, unlike anything I could remember. Did I know about this once?

She touched my chin and brought my eyes to meet hers. I could feel soothing energy emanating from her.

"Most of the physical wounds were easy to repair, but the rest, the magical and emotional, may take more determination on your part. Your magic suffered but will return. I fear your ability to reproduce is diminished from the damage. I know your lineage and the significance that news brings. However, you may be able to overcome all of that if others can aid you more than we can do here," she said.

It wasn't horrible news, not to one who had never thought she wanted to have children, but at the same time, it landed like a pit in my stomach. What if that was the only way to secure the legacy of my family's treasured book?

I nodded. "Again, thank you. Who are you, and why? I mean, how do I deserve such aid? How can I be of service to you after all that you have done for me."

"Who we are is unimportant other than we are here to assist you. We are lucky our little friends found you and took a liking to you. Even they are not safe with the hunters around," she said.

A small creature flew into the tent, hovering next to the doorway. The white lady extended her hand, and it landed on her, then crawled up and sat on her shoulder. It appeared to be a small golden dragon.

"There is much change and much more to come. If we follow the right path, it can benefit those of us who are now in the most danger. More than that, I cannot say at this time. There is much for you to discover now that you have returned here. I think you will find things unfolding faster than anticipated."

Why no one would just spell things out for me was frustrating, but for some reason, I felt no desire to cross-examine her. The love I felt shining forth from her was so comforting. Part of me wanted to stay here. It felt so safe. But at the same time, I knew I had more to learn, more to do, more to discover. Whether it was Lazlo's family issues or my own, I was needed.

"Am I well enough to return?" I asked.

I worried about Lazlo; sure, he was more than capable, but what if waiting for me compromised his safety?

"Yes, I do believe your body has recovered enough that you are not in immediate danger to proceed, so I will take you back to where you were, with he who is watching out for you," she said.

She took my hand again, and the bright glow intensified between, through, and around us. When at last I could see, I was back in the woods. Lazlo stood before me. He took my hand, and we began to walk away.

"Mage," the white lady called after Lazlo. He turned to her. "They are seeking this one. So many are seeking this one. Some mean you both harm, some only harm to one of you. Others are your friends. Be cautious."

She disappeared. Suddenly Lazlo grabbed my hand and pulled me behind a tree, signaling me to stay quiet.

A man was running toward where we were. "I smelt it, my Lord, I know I did. It was up here somewhere. Stronger than I ever smelt in my life. A magic creature I know it, not even human, like it was almost all magic." The little man was smelling the air as if he were a dog on a hunt. He looked rather absurd in my mind.

The man behind him was elegantly dressed, very upper-class looking, and seemed disdainful of the smelling man.

"Well, catch it for me already then, or let's go back and let someone else do this. I'm tired of walking on dead leaves. This whole outdoors thing is beneath me."

I could see a mischievous grin cross Lazlo's face as he surveyed the scene and tested the air with his hand. A flick of his wrist and a large black horse, looking as if it had just lost its rider, came charging at the two men. The well-dressed one yelped and jumped away, and the small sniffer man attempted to jump onto the horse's back. He failed and landed flat on his face in the dirt. The horse then slowed and went over to the aristocrat, who slowly peered at it.

The small man was wide-eyed. "Look, M'Lord, it likes you. The magical horse likes you?"

The aristocrat smirked and shook his head. "Of course he likes me, you dolt. This is *my* horse. You might have tied him up properly as I told you to!" He quickly mounted, clearly intending to ride off.

"But my Lord, there is magic here, I swear it!"

"Oh, I'm supposed to believe the idiot who can't even properly tie up a horse? No, thank you. I'm going back to camp. You can find your own way."

He galloped off, leaving the small man looking dejected. He looked around, wearily hung his head, and followed in the same direction the horse and rider had gone.

Questions

We watched them disappear into the distance before Lazlo allowed any movement. Now that my mind felt clearer, I was evaluating this different man before me. Seeing him in this new element. I was intrigued. Who was this man? He had many attributes I was unaware of, and I wondered what else was beneath the surface.

"He's far enough away now. We're in the clear." He led me forward, away from where we'd seen the two men go. "That blast of magic that brought you back must have triggered him and also blinded him as to our magics. I don't know what has brought them this far North. Magic hunting is illegal, but not all of the kingdoms do much to prevent it."

"Evidently I've much to learn if I'm to navigate this place successfully," I said.

My mind was back on mission. Seeing Gwen had to be next. I knew I was almost at my destination when I'd been taken from the train.

"Agreed. For now, we need to get back to the manor. Already I've been gone too long, but the risk was necessary. I'm unsure how much time I have to get back. I must perform the rituals as soon as possible." He looked in my eyes as if evaluating me. "You seem better. How do you feel? I was terribly worried about you."

I nodded. "Better, not on fire, not vomiting. Nothing is aching. Fine actually. So talk to me as we walk, tell me anything else I need to know. I still want to find your sister and talk to her. It's an important piece of the puzzle."

Lazlo shook his head. "No, not on your own, I can't; I won't allow you to risk yourself like that again."

"Then find me an escort you can trust in the next town up ahead if that makes you feel better. Pay them or let me pay them to escort me if necessary, but let me do this while you return home and take care of what only you can do. I'm going one way or another."

Lazlo let out a sound that was half sigh, half chuckle. "Is this what I have to look forward to if you finally consent to be my partner? You're not an easy one to bargain with," he said. He looked at me and smiled, softly shaking his head. "We'll go into this town up ahead, and I'll scout out an escort. I still have contacts here that will help. But if we can't find anyone that meets my standards of reliability, you come back with me, where I can protect you, and I'll get you an escort there to help you go out again, agreed?"

"I suppose, but we're so close already. At least I think we are. It would be a shame to go all the way back and then have to make this same trip again." It seemed logical to accept his bargain. I didn't want to face being kidnapped and possibly sold again. He stopped in his tracks and turned to me.

"Nothing - I mean nothing - is more important than your life and your safety Marjorie. I'm the one who invited you here. You are my responsibility. I never intended to send you out on your own, although I thought it would be safer than it turned out to be. I've been out of circulation for too long."

"Isn't Gwen in danger from these groups of men?"

"Her magic is dormant. They can only smell active magics. Otherwise, I'd be on my way to her with you right now. Knowing what we know now, you can't use any of your magic when you're with her. That's too dangerous with these groups so close by."

"Why were you able to use magic back there? I couldn't do anything at all when they grabbed me. That was how you brought the horse in, wasn't it?"

"Yes, but under the circumstances, I felt it was an acceptable risk, a distraction to draw them away from us. The sniffers, as we refer to them, cannot block magic, only detect it. Besides, there was no need to spill any more blood unless our lives depended on it."

He said that statement so matter of fact as if it wasn't that unusual of an occurrence. I thought about the carnage at the cabin. The ease with which he struck them down, no hesitation. He'd been ruthless. It was clear that wasn't the first time he'd struck people down with a sword. He was built broad and muscular, a man of substantial physical power. He didn't need to rely on magic to defend himself.

"Where'd you learn to do it, to fight like that? I didn't think mages were warriors. Certainly not any I've ever met"

"My father was a general in King Ceffert's army and well known for his skills. I enlisted and also served."

"You were in the King's army?"

"Yes, for several years. Mother was certain I'd not grow up to be that much of a magician. It was Gwen who held that destiny. So Gwen was taught magic, and I was taught fighting. Granted, we both learned to defend ourselves with both magic and fighting skills, but I had substantially more of one, and she had substantially more of the other."

"So what about now? With Gwen gone?"

"When she gave up her inheritance, all the ancestral magic passed to me, as much as we have access to currently since Mother is still alive anyway. Mother holds the true power of the manor."

"Was your father a mage as well as a warrior?"

"He was of magical lineage, as well as being a well-respected warrior. That is the case with most of my relatives on his side. They aren't mages but are magically inclined."

"So how often do you have to... I mean, defend yourself like that?"

"I can honestly say I've never had to cut down six men in one day before when it wasn't in the middle of a battle. I take no joy in ending lives, but when it comes to men such as those, I've made the mistake of attempting to bargain with them in the past, and I won't do it again."

He killed those people to protect me. The idea that it had been at all necessary was frightening. The cabin's events were feeling more like a dream as we walked, and I was thankful I was no longer in any sort of pain.

Our walk was rather pleasant, considering the circumstances. Lazlo was being forthcoming, telling me whatever I asked and not quizzing me about anything. The forest ended, and before us was a meadow. There was a town on the other side of it.

"Come. Let's go into town. I know the blacksmith here. He's made weapons for me; actually, I bought this knife from him. He may be able to help us find someone to escort you."

The mention of the knife sent me back to the cabin. The image flashed in my mind of the gang leader running for me and being brought down by Lazlo's swift action. Lazlo pulling that knife out of the slumped body and cleaning it off was also an image burned in my brain.

As much as I was feeling more myself, that flash and the pain in my heart that came with it made me realize what the white lady had meant, I might be able to function, to set that trauma aside, but it still lingered. All the same, I was composed enough to carry it with me, seeing it and knowing it was there without falling apart or letting on in any way to Lazlo.

The Escort

We made our way into the town with ease. No one seemed to pay much attention to us as strangers, although the women we passed were staring and pointing as Lazlo walked by. I got the sense he was somewhat known here. When we hit the market area, Lazlo went straight for the blacksmith's shop. A booming voice greeted us from the shadows.

"Well, well well, aren't you a sight for sore eyes! Been far too long, Lazlo of Ealach." A bald man with enormous forearms and respectable muscles of his own appeared and extended his large hand to Lazlo. The two men exchanged a hearty, forceful handshake.

"And who might this charming lady by your side be? Did you finally marry, Lazlo?"

"Eldrich, I'd like you to meet Marjorie. We're passing through town but have urgent business. I need to find her an escort, someone trustworthy and capable of helping her travel safely through this region. Can you help us?" It didn't miss my attention that he failed to answer that other question at all.

"Oooh, did I hear Mister Lazlo is here?" From the back of the shop, a small but very voluptuous woman appeared, grinning widely.

"Lazlo, you remember my wife, Midge. Midge, this fine lady with Lazlo is Marjorie."

"Lovely name for a lovely girl. All the girls in town will be so disappointed. They've already been chattering that he came in town with a woman on his arm. You've snatched a good one, Lady Marjorie. So many others have tried to get or keep his attention."

I didn't know what to say - correct her or just go with it. After all, technically, we were promised to each other. I suddenly realized I didn't like other women gawking at him. It was Lazlo who spoke up.

"Marjorie is indeed a special lady to me, but if you must know, we are not married, so please give her some space there if you don't mind."

"Oooh, Eldrich, he's still not married. I may leave you yet for this charmer." She tapped Lazlo on the shoulder, and he laughed.

"Think twice about that one, Lazlo; she's a handful." He grinned at his wife, who was flirting back at him. They were an adorable couple, and it was evident that they enjoyed joking with each other, but their love was deep. It shone from their faces.

"Well, friends, if we are done discussing my eligibility, can we discuss my business?" Lazlo asked.

"Only if you both join us for dinner, you and your 'special' woman," Midge said with a wink.

Lazlo nodded. "We'd be delighted."

The conversation turned to news of the town since Lazlo's last visit. The discussion led us to dinner. Midge was an excellent cook, and I was far hungrier than I'd realized. The recommended escort was due back in town in the morning. Lazlo looked uneasy at the thought of staying another night but seemed to have no intention of budging.

After sharing the meal with the couple, we checked into a room at a local tavern. As we began to settle in, Lazlo created a space on the floor next to the bed. My heart was heavy. Perhaps I did repulse him now.

"I'll be right here. Keeping you safe." He said.

I nodded and began to slide under the covers. Then I sat up. I had to know what I didn't want to know.

"Do you not want me anymore? Do I repulse you?" For some reason, the panic was gripping my throat.

His eyes widened. He moved to sit next to me on the bed. "Marjorie," he stroked my hair, "nothing could be further from the truth. You've been through so much. I thought that space would serve you better."

"But you told her you were single. So now all the women in town who want you . . ." I trailed off, giving in to my tears.

Lazlo stroked my hair. "Well, the last time I checked, I was single. Do you want to marry me?"

"No," I sobbed. "Well, maybe."

He chuckled lightly, amused, and surprised. "Maybe, huh?"

Our eyes met. I lurched forward and kissed him. His responsive kiss was gentle, loving, and sweet, but I wanted him. I wanted sex on my terms, hoping that that would wash away some of the emptiness I felt.

As we kissed, I traced my hand down his chest, across his muscled stomach, but as I shifted my hand below his naval, he pulled his lips from mine, our foreheads touching. He lifted my hand and placed my hand firmly on his chest. I could feel his heart beating rapidly.

"At this moment, know that I want you. I truly do. The feel of you, the smell of you, is so intoxicating. I can't lose you because I didn't say no when I should have. Besides, I think sleep should be first on your agenda for tonight. You have healing to do," he said.

"How many other girlfriends have you had?"

"What?" he asked.

"How many other girlfriends have you had? Other women you were involved with?"

"For someone who wanted me to have sex with her a moment ago, you seem intent on breaking any possible mood," he said.

"And you seem hesitant to give me an answer."

"Other girlfriends? Let's see if I was to say your question is other than you, then are you saying that you consider yourself my girlfriend?" he asked.

His distraction game was in high gear. I had to laugh.

"Well, maybe," I said.

"At least you didn't start that one with a no," he said.

He leaned back in, touching my face, tracing my hair. He kissed my forehead.

"As far as I'm concerned, I am yours, know that."

I was melting into his arms again. Being with him felt so comfortable, so right. I nestled my head against his chest and quickly fell asleep.

******

"Eh hem," someone loudly voiced from inside the room, startling me awake. Lazlo immediately pushed himself in front of me.

"Geez Lazlo, sorry I startled you, but you can't expect me to wait all day while you snooze"

Lazlo's tension dropped. He'd been ready to spring at the

stranger in the doorway. A tall, slender woman donned in leather, sword on her hip stood there, looking at us.

"Ana. As I live and breathe, I certainly didn't expect to see you. A whirling warrior? Really? I'd never have guessed that choice," he said.

There was a hint of sarcasm in his voice.

For some odd reason, my brain was swirling. This woman had some sort of a history with him. I wasn't sure about this.

"Marjorie, I'd like you to meet Ana," Lazlo said as he got out of bed, still fully dressed from the night before. "She trained with Father, and with me. She and Gwen were also dear friends for many years."

"Not past tense. Gwen and I just took different paths. The love of our sisterhood is still there. Yesterday when Eldrich threw me a connection that it was you seeking an escort, I knew I wanted to come," she said.

She pulled an apple out of her bag, examining it as she spoke.

"Then I was excited to hear this escort you need was taking someone to see your sister. At least, that's what Eldrich told me when I woke him up as soon as I got back into town. When he told me you were staying in this tavern, I decided not to delay,"

She crunched into the apple she held in her hand. Her stance was casual; her aura of confidence said she feared very little.

"When Eldrich spoke of someone, he never mentioned it was anyone I knew. Then again . . ."

"Exactly; he had no idea we knew each other. It was purely the will of the Goddess that drew us together. Another reason I knew I had to be the one."

In my brief time here, this was the first time I'd heard anyone mention any deity. My curiosity was peaked but interrupting seemed, well, rude at this point.

"Apologies, Marjorie. I hope you can forgive this lug here for ignoring you momentarily. Sometimes he just stands there being all muscles and handsome and forgets his manners," Ana said, punching him lightly in the shoulder.

Lazlo seemed a little irritated, took the jabs, and merely sighed. I sensed him wanting to object but then letting it go.

"Let's go downstairs and discuss this over breakfast, shall we?" Lazlo turned to me. "I want you to decide for yourself if this is an arrangement with which you are comfortable. For my part, any member of the whirling warriors is an adequate escort, more than capable of defending you should the need arise."

"Be comfortable?" I said quietly to Lazlo as we headed down the stairs out of the room. "Is she a past girlfriend? Did you two ever . . .?"

"Oh hell no," Ana proclaimed, heading down the stairs before Lazlo could say a word.

"I mean comfortable as in you feeling safe, nothing more," Lazlo said.

We arrived in the tavern and sat at a table. Ana seemed to be giving me a stern look over.

"Lazlo, why don't you go over there and just look pretty for a while. Us women need to chat alone."

"Marjorie..?" Lazlo leveled his eyes at me, checking in before agreeing to anything.

I nodded. "I'll be fine," I said.

He stood up and backed away from the table, his eyes on Ana the whole time. Then he took a seat at the bar area and began to engage in conversation with the man behind the counter.

I was uncertain exactly what Lazlo's unease was; he knew

this woman and seemed to have some level of trust in her. Was he afraid she'd say something to me he didn't want me to know or hear?

"I get the sense you aren't from around here. That you aren't familiar with our ways, would you say that is accurate?" Ana asked.

I nodded and said, "Good assessment." I wasn't sure how much to offer up, so keeping things brief seemed best.

"No need for details, simply information that I need if I'm going to keep you safe on this journey," she said.

A young woman approached our table. "Can I get you ladies anything? The gentleman over there said to get you whatever you wanted." She motioned to Lazlo.

Ana smiled. "Now that you mention it, I'm starving."

The two of them conversed, and once things were decided, the young woman left. Ana turned back to me.

"For the most part, magic users are respected or even revered here, but there's been unrest of late. Factions are building up of non-magic people. Many have been convinced that magic is the root of all their troubles."

"What's their reason for that? I've seen magic help a lot of people."

"One mage, years ago. He did a lot of damage."

"Malek?" I asked. I'd read stories of him, the scarring he caused to the land.

She nodded. "Because of it, mutations have surfaced. Some prevent magic from being used. Another common mutation causes an ability to smell magic that isn't in the earth or plant life. They often join together. I'm guessing you encountered one of this gangs for Lazlo to be this far from the manor. Something you couldn't deal with on your own - though I can sense you are formidable in your own right with magic."

"Yes. If Lazlo hadn't found me, I'm not sure I'd still be alive," I said.

"It was foolishly trusting of him to send you out alone in the first place. The man has been too sheltered since his sister left. Much has been going on in those few years."

The young woman returned to the table with several plates of food and set them on the table. Ana excitedly began to dig in.

"Are you in touch with Gwen at all these days?"

She shook her head. "Not for some time, sadly. I've been training, and I've only recently been sanctioned to travel in my order, so I've only just now returned to the area. But back to your boyfriend." She waved her fork toward Lazlo.

Boyfriend? That sounded strange.

"He is your boyfriend, isn't he? I figure if he'd gotten married, that news would've traveled. So you do like him, you want to be with him, right? The way he looks at you like he's guarding his sacred prize, I can see how *he* feels," she said.

"What difference does it make?" I asked.

"I won't return you to him unless that's your will. If he expects me to do so simply because he demands it, he's wrong. Lazlo can be persuasive and demanding. He wants what he wants." Her eyes scanned me. She leaned back in her chair. "However, I sense something between the two of you, which tells me that it isn't an issue. I merely want to understand before you and I take off together if I'll have to cross him in the end. I'd prefer not to cross him without foreknowledge."

I glanced over at Lazlo, his muscular form leaning against the counter as he watched us from that distance while occasionally chatting with others in the tavern.

"He is . . . just so . . ."

"Stubborn? Impossible? Fucking hot? All of them work and are commonly used to describe him, depending on who you are. Which were you going for?"

There it was again. I had to speak up. "You seem fixated on his appearance. You've called him handsome, pretty, and hot, all in this short time."

Ana laughed and shook her head. "Calm down. I can see how people respond to him. Besides, he hates it, and I've always loved irritating him. Admittedly it's been a long time since I've had the opportunity. But back to you, your role in all of this. What is it that *you* want?"

At that moment, I was less sure of what I wanted than I'd been in most of my life. Looking over at him, feeling what I felt in his presence, it turned virtually everything I'd ever thought I wanted upside down.

"I want to help Lazlo break the hold the manor has on him. That's why I'm seeking Gwen. She has information that Lazlo doesn't that could help."

"And their Mother? You know about her, right?"

"He told me that was a major part of him wanting to be able to travel away from the manor to find her and get their family, er issues, settled."

Ana nodded. My answer seemed acceptable. "Okay, got it. So then, before Mr. Impatient over there stomps back here, are you and I good? Do you trust me?"

"Yes, I think we're good." Lazlo did look like he was about to break a piece from that counter; his gaze upon us had intensified. For my part, I just wanted someone reliable with me, so that I could accomplish the mission. Ana seemed like she'd do the trick.

Ana signaled him over, and he wasted no time taking a seat next to me at the table.

"Your lady and I have agreed. I'll take her to Gwen and escort her back to you, or as close as you'll allow me," Ana said.

Ana moved the plate of bread toward him. He shook his head and scooted it back toward her.

"Signal me when you're nearing the train station, and I'll send my driver to collect her." His eyes turned to me. "Marjorie, I'll look forward to having you safely back with me. I have faith in Ana's abilities, but I wish it could be me with you. I'd feel much better if it were." He glanced anxiously at the door. "I fear something is amiss, and I must make haste in getting back home. I should've felt a strong pull by now, but I don't, and that itself is alarming. Be safe, both of you."

He looked into my eyes. Each of us seemed unsure of what was expected of the other. I didn't want him to go. I heard him growl under his breath. He grabbed me, pulling me to him and kissing me. His kiss was deliberate, passionate, and I felt it was for the benefit of the eyes of all those surrounding us.

He pulled away, and it felt as if all the air had left the room, or at least my lungs.

"I'll be waiting for you," he said as he got up and walked away.

My eyes followed his form, my heart racing as I watched him exit the room. I turned to Ana, who was grinning. She shrugged. "He is a complicated man. But girl, you just got *tagged*. No man for miles around here will dare bother you once the rumors fly, and all those women with eyeballs on him will know their chances are sunk."

"If he rarely leaves the manor, how does he get such a reputation?"

"He left plenty when he wasn't the only one there. Only

one of them needs to be nearby. The family itself has quite a reputation." She moved another plate of food in front of me. "C'mon, let's finish up breakfast and get moving. We've got a train to catch," she said.

Sisterhood

Our journey to the station was uneventful. Once we boarded the train, I continued to press Ana for information about this realm. A lot of what she shared was local politics. This king did this, that queen did that, none of it made much sense. Still, I now had a clearer understanding of the magic versus non-magics and their relationship. As the train slowed to a stop, Ana signaled that this was our destination.

While we walked through the train station and toward the road, people were staring. I wondered why since I didn't feel I looked that unusual, but perhaps it was Ana by my side, a tall blonde in her leather warrior gear with an above average confidence in her stride. I hoped we wouldn't attract much attention, even if we were an odd-looking pair.

Once we were clear of the train station, I could see a nearby town further down the dirt road. Ana pointed.

"That's where we'll find her and her family. Her husband's a good soul. Gwen adores him. It's only a short walk, no sense in hiring a lift."

Ana ushered me out of the street to make way for a horse and carriage passing by. She pointed to a small dirt street. As we ventured there, the town center gave way to a small grouping of homes. Chickens were hopping in the streets, and an older woman was rushing out to chase them. From across the street, a woman shouted,

"I told you to upgrade your pen Thela! Darion would have sold you a better one."

The older woman threw a disgusted glance at her, and when my eyes followed, I knew it was Gwen. Her smile was so much like Lazlo's. She looked at the woman fumbling over her chicken and laughed. Her hair was not as blonde as I remembered and had developed a reddish hue, but there was no mistaking her. She'd grown up to be a stunning woman, tall and slender with large eyes and a face as beautiful as her brother's. I glanced at Ana, who was smiling broadly.

"Excuse me," Ana shouted in a bizarre accent as she waved at Gwen. "Would you be so kind as to help me with some directions?"

Gwen's eyes widened, her jaw dropped.

She said nothing but waved us frantically toward her house. As we got to the porch, she yelped and threw her arms around Ana. "What in holy hell are you doing here? I thought you were still locked away in a tower training day in and day out."

"I got my stars just a few weeks ago. Then the other day, as I was headed toward Grevl, I got a message from Eldrich, the blacksmith, that your brother was seeking a seasoned warrior to escort his girlfriend around. The icing on the cake was when I found out I was supposed to take her to see you!"

Gwen's eyes turned to me. "Lazlo's girlfriend?"

A look of disbelief crossed her face, then eyes wide, and with her jaw dropping again, she said, "Marjorie? Is that you? After all this time?"

I nodded my head.

"Well, please ladies, come inside."

We proceeded into her modest but comfortable home. The front room was more like the places I was accustomed to living, much more modest than her grand family home.

"Darion!" She called out to her husband. A handsome, friendly face peered out from the back door.

"Yes, my love?"

"We have visitors. You remember Ana, and this is Marjorie, an old friend. The three of us need some undisturbed ladies talk time, so can you keep the toddlers at bay?"

"Of course. I'll see to Shelei and Marda and make sure they are sufficiently entertained."

"Thank you," they exchanged a sweet kiss before he disappeared into their upper floor. Gwen watched him before turning to me. There was fire in her eyes.

"So what the hell? It's been twelve years. Where have you been? Why didn't you at least tell Laz something? And he just took you back instantly? After you disappeared on him?" Gwen said.

Lazlo may have hinted at hurt at my disappearance, but he'd never directly accused me of hurting him. Her words landed hard.

"I . . .I'm sorry. I don't remember any of it."

"Now that's convenient," Gwen said

"I don't. I don't know what happened. I don't know why Gran and I left. I remember some pieces of earlier life here but nothing about that last year."

"Really? You don't remember anything that happened? I'm sorry, but that's just strange. It'd take a unique mage to remove memories selectively. Unless it's some special potion in your book?"

"Not one I've ever seen."

She paused, just looking at me, sizing me up. She looked at Ana. Ana shrugged.

"Wait, you said you met Laz in Grevl? What was he doing so far away from the manor?" Gwen asked.

"Rescuing this one from some nasty types," Ana replied, pointing to me.

"Magic sniffers, I'd wager," Gwen said. Ana nodded. "I hadn't heard they were in these parts, but they are a growing problem. I hope Laz cut them down." Gwen looked at me. "That had to be awful. You were lucky, not many get captured and are ever heard from again."

The smell and touch of the men, the image of the bloody floor, Lazlo's gleaming blade again flashed in my head.

"I'd rather not discuss it if you don't mind," I said. The tension I felt building in my body at the mention of those men was reminder enough.

"You don't have to twist my arm to change *that* subject," Gwen said. "So, are you and Laz finally getting married? Did you come to invite me to the wedding? He did ask, didn't he?"

"Um, well, yes, he made that offer, but, no. I came because Lazlo wants to dismantle the gate. I want to help him." I said.

"Oh, so you're here about my amulet. That makes sense. You really don't remember, do you?"

"No, please enlighten me."

"You helped me create that piece. At the time, you were in line to be my sister-in-law."

"The books said nothing about me."

"Well, I didn't exactly tell Mother I had help. If you read the journals, you know the properties and why, at least currently, you can't use it."

"Because I'm not family."

"Exactly."

"But where is it? I've searched your old room and found nothing."

"That's where it gets interesting. I placed a spell on it before I left. It'll appear to whoever accepted Laz's proposal. The first part of it anyway. The rest of it attaches after he's married. It should work, but it hasn't been tested. Laz hasn't gotten engaged to anyone since our parents disappeared."

"So he's been engaged before?"

"Oh Lord, yes. Mother tried to get him married at least half a dozen times. Laz was sure you'd come back, so he refused to set aside your original contract. That meant that any woman he did marry risked him being allowed to set her aside if you returned and wanted him to honor your contract. Kind of a hard sell."

"So he's never been married?" I asked.

"Nope. Mother gave up. Of course, she still had me so she wasn't that worried. Obviously, things are different now." Gwen said.

"Well, if we can dismantle that gate, it won't matter."

Gwen shrugged. "Except that you can't dismantle it without a piece that you can't use unless you marry my brother."

"There has to be another way."

"There's a different tool. The cloak pin Father wore would be something Laz could use to amplify his power."

"Where would that be?"

"Wherever Father is. Unless Mother has it. Either way, not doing Laz much good."

This wasn't going as smoothly as I'd hoped. "So you are saying we're out of luck?" Her eyes locked on the crystal around my neck. "You can summon Laz, see if he has any other ideas. I'd love to see him, and it would be good for all of us to chat together."

Ana held up a hand and twisted a ring on her finger. I sensed an energetic bubble form around us. "A dark spot so no one will detect the use of magic here," she stated.

I placed my hand on the crystal and concentrated on summoning Lazlo. I was unsure how this would work. Gwen seemed to know more than I did.

As soon as he appeared in a somewhat ethereal form, Gwen called out, "Laz!"

"Gwen? Are you with Marjorie? Is that why you can see me?"

"Of course, silly. I've missed your brutish face."

"And I've missed your sarcastic wit. Dear sister, I fear I cannot chat at present, and I request that Marjorie returns to me with the best possible speed. I hope your visit has been productive. And so lovely that the two of you got to meet up and chat." With that, he went dark.

"Well, that was weird," Ana managed.

"Gwen, honey, I could use some help here!" We heard a cry for assistance from her husband upstairs.

"I'll be up in a minute, sweetie," she shouted up the stairs before turning to me. "I'll give you the location of a nearby mage." She scribbled on a nearby piece of paper. "You can decide if you want to try him or if you're going back right away as Laz requested. I know Ana can look out for you, and that likely you are more than capable yourself, even if Laz is overly protective." She handed me the paper, grabbing my hand as she did. "He adores you; he always has," she said. I nodded.

Gwen had added a new layer of perspective to my thoughts regarding Lazlo. I had much to consider.

"Ana, I truly wish you could stay awhile. Come back when you can," Gwen said.

"Goddess willing," Ana said as she and Gwen embraced.

With that, we took our leave of her and headed back to the train station.

A Family Affair

Before deciding which direction to go, I opened the paper to see what Gwen had written. To my surprise, the named mage was one I had met before in New York. He had shared with me additional details of the spell caster of my book. Perhaps he had other knowledge that could help us that wasn't in those family books.

"Ana, this mage Gwen mentioned, he may have information that could be quite helpful, and he isn't far away."

Ana looked stern. "I don't want to scare you, but something is wrong. Lazlo would never cut out on his sister like that. He kept that session extremely brief, mentioning only you and Gwen, and if I'm right, someone was listening or maybe even watching. He didn't want them to know I was there too or know exactly where Gwen was either." She began to walk faster.

"But he asked me to come back right away. So it can't be that dangerous, not with the lengths he has gone to, to protect me so far."

"True, but it could be danger he feels he can protect you from if you're with him but not if you're apart. Plus, he knows I'm sneaking up there. No way I'm not. Hand me that crystal, will you?"

I complied, unsure what this plan might be.

Ana brought out a small knife and cut it into the crystal until a small chip fell off into her hand. "That'll be enough to get me there. It'll guide me and keep me from falling off the road if that fog protection is active."

We collected our tickets and boarded the next appropriate train to head back to the manor. On the ride back, my mind was racing. What was so important. If he turned out to be simply overprotective, then I'd be pissed. But it hadn't seemed like that, and with Ana's concerns, I worried even more.

I exited the train alone. Ana had disappeared. I was met again at the station by Arthur in the carriage. Arthur seemed more subdued than when I'd last seen him. I attempted conversation, but he seemed lost in another world. Still, he dutifully took me up to the manor as before. The carriage stopped, and Arthur opened the door.

I was met by the sight of a tall, buxom redheaded woman standing at the entrance of the manor. She was dressed in a jeweled jade gown that emphasized her voluptuous figure. Her hair was thick and full and almost wild but still perfectly coiffed. She was a perfect presentation of beauty and sensuality mixed with pride and ambition. An aura of power unlike any I'd ever seen before radiated from her and surrounded her. The beautifully defined face-shape told me all I needed to know. Both Gwen and Lazlo had inherited aspects of that sculpted face. Even if I didn't remember her quite like this, there was no denying that this was their mother, Maeve.

"Hello Marjorie, I'm so glad you came. Lazlo told me you'd been here and were planning on coming to see him again. Poor boy just can't keep anything from *me,* you know. Well, don't just stand there; we've got planning to do. Come inside."

I wondered where Lazlo was and what had she'd done to him? As we walked through the entrance hall, there was an altar placed in the center. In the middle was a horrifying sight. Two young children - or what remained of them - were in the center. The bodies looked to be lifeless at first glance. There was blood everywhere, but then the two heads turned, eyes dead but watching and waiting patiently. But for what, I had no idea. Horrifyingly, one screeched and pointed at me. I jumped as terror filled my body.

"Now, now, child. Calm down," Maeve said to it. She turned to me."Pay no mind to them; they just identify pretty things like you."

That was all she offered me.

She led me into the kitchen. Lazlo, seated at the table, abruptly rose as I entered. "Marjorie, I'm sorry to bring you here like this."

Maeve leaned in and whispered in my ear, "No, he is not; he loves having you here. That's why I made sure he brought you." She turned to Lazlo. "Don't you have an important matter to ask Marjorie about?"

"Mother, please. This isn't necessary."

"Yes, Lazlo, it is *quite* necessary due to your more lengthy stay away from home. So careless that the manor called for *me*." She shot him a glare. He averted his eyes from her. "Convenient for you that the woman you were promised to, the one you wanted, was so accessible. You get what your heart desires, and so do I. Finally, once and for all, I will be rid of this place."

"But Mother . . ."

She shook her head. "If it weren't for you and your gentleman's agreement, this would already be done. Her family already said yes. Now be a good boy and do as you are told."

Her tone was cold and commanding.

Lazlo looked back at her, sighed, and moved in front of me, and got down on one knee.

"Marjorie, I know I promised not to ask again this soon, but the fates are dictating otherwise, so I'm asking again now. Will you consent to be my bride?"

What the hell was I to do? If I said yes, that amulet stone would appear in Lazlo's hand whether or not he knew it. But marry him? I felt as if my back was up against the wall; up ahead, I could see a cliff that I just wanted to jump off and get away from here. How many times had I balked at this very thing?

My mind was racing as he knelt there for what felt like an eternity. Then I looked into his eyes, fell into their beauty. I could see his love behind them. I realized I could love him, that I did love him. But forever?

Maeve grew impatient at my silence.

"Well, don't leave him down there in misery too long. Either say yes and seal the deal or say no, nullify the contract, and walk away from here for good. He gave you a choice, which is more than he should be doing. My son needs a bride, so it's you, or I'll find him someone else."

Someone else. Those words rolled through my head.

Lazlo had averted his eyes from me. If I said no, I'd be unable to help him. I'd also lose him. Maeve would make sure of it. This was a frightening decision for me, but losing him wasn't what I wanted. That much I knew. I reached to his face and turned his eyes to meet mine. I took a deep breath to gain my courage.

"Yes, I consent to be your bride," I said.

Lazlo sighed, half smiled, and shook his head slightly. He was visibly relieved those moments of torment were over. Maeve turned away to grab a celebratory glass as Lazlo became aware of what he held in his hand; our eyes remained locked, and he quickly pocketed the jewel before she noticed.

"Well, get up. Finally, you're going to get married. She's a tad unusual, always has been, but we'll make the best of it. At least the family contract will finally be fulfilled."

Unusual? The girl on the train had said, "interesting." I hadn't seen many different people here, but I was beginning to feel even more like an outsider with comments like those.

Lazlo shook his head and mouthed, "I'm sorry" to me. I reached out and grabbed his hand, signaling my acceptance.

Foreign Rituals

Maeve beckoned us into the great room of the manor and waved her hands. Light sprung before her, and there was a vibrant flash. Suddenly the gruesome scene from moments before had vanished from the entryway, and there were elaborate decorations everywhere. Instantly I found myself clothed in a white gown and Lazlo in elegant formal wear. Maeve's magic moved him across the room, away from me.

I felt panic scrambling in my brain. When I'd said yes, I hadn't been thinking right *now*. I shoved it aside. We'd get through this; we'd find a way to free Maeve and dismantle the gate. We'd do it together. I'd deal with this whole marriage thing.

There were ethereal forms, some more solid than others, all present, some sitting in chairs, others standing by. A ghostly priest was at the front, standing next to Lazlo.

This was far more magic than I'd ever seen at once in my life. The power and knowledge required to do this were off the charts. Maeve was more formidable than anyone I'd ever seen. I heard her in a chair in the front row speaking to a spirit.

"After all these years, *finally* he's getting married," she said, offering the ghost a tissue. The tissue dropped to the floor, and the spirit pretended to weep. 'Yes, I know, you always cried at weddings," Maeve said to the spirit.

Music was playing, and my feet moved as if on their own up the aisle. I wanted to resist. I desperately wanted to run. This whole scene was so insane. Before I could come to terms with it I was face to face with Lazlo, and the ghostly priest connected our hands. As he began the ceremony, his words evaporated as Lazlo and I locked eyes. I found he was inside my head.

"Don't flinch or let on that you can hear me. She was here when I returned. She opened the gateway, and most of the ancestors are loose, although she has kept them here on the grounds. This is the only safe way for us to communicate. Blink twice if Ana is coming"

I blinked twice; after all, she had said she was coming, but I hadn't a clue where she was.

Lazlo silenced his thoughts as the priest addressed us, and it became necessary for us to play our parts in the ceremony, reciting the vows he gave us. When he pronounced us married, Lazlo pulled me into him and kissed me gently and tenderly, almost apologetically. I felt a delicate chain and the weight of a small stone materialize around my neck. I brought a finger to it and whispered a spell to hide its presence.

Maeve stood up and applauded. It was the oddest wedding I'd ever seen, and it was mine. Oddly, that seemed as logical as it was terrifying.

Maeve greeted us at the end of the aisle as we walked out. "Congratulations, you two. Oh, such a relief!" She placed a hand on Lazlo's shoulder. "You are finally married, and to the sweet girl you wanted all those years ago. How lovely."

"Mother, is there an event we need to attend or are we allowed to retire together?"

Maeve nodded. "Go on upstairs. You know what you need to do, son. Once you're officially locked in as Lord and Lady of this estate and I'm free, then I'll leave you two alone. More or less, anyway."

Lazlo gripped my hand with a reassuring squeeze. "Thank you, Mother," he said before leading me up the stairs.

Lazlo's silent message was in my head again.

"Rest assured someone is listening, someone who will report to her, so this silent speech is our best way. Please believe me, even though ultimately this is what I'd sought, I had no hand in it. I need you to know that. I wanted you to come to this agreement on your terms."

I found I could reply to him now without speaking. *"Ana said I couldn't refuse her, that she was coming whether I asked her to or not. That's all I know. Gwen told me that amulet stone would appear in your hand when you proposed, and I accepted. I took the risk that Maeve wouldn't see it. But now that we are married, and once we figure out how to use it, I'll be able to use its power. Together we can drive them all back."*

"So you agreed solely to that purpose?" His thought sounded hurt, but what else could I say?

"You know marriage wasn't on my agenda. Still, I knew if I didn't agree, I'd have lost you forever. I knew that wasn't my desire."

He squeezed my hand. *"I'm glad to hear that. I hope you are feeling alright now. About me. About us. Despite this oddity. There is more we need to do tonight. Please just trust me."*

We'd made it to Lazlo's bedroom by this time. There was a feeling I'd been in this room before, but the memory felt just out of reach. When he spoke out loud, it was almost startling to hear his voice again after our silent conversation.

"There is a ritual to this. A ritual of our joining. Unfortunately, I was unable to have the time to prepare you, so please just trust me and do as I guide you."

I figured consummating our marriage just meant having sex after we said our vows, but apparently, there was more to this. Lazlo was getting undressed and signaled for me to do the same.

"Come, place your hands on mine."

I did as he requested, still unsure what was about to happen.

"Close your eyes."

As soon as I closed my eyes, I felt it. Energy was flowing through him into me. Unlike the ceremony we had just been through, this was a ritual magical union.

The energy was surrounding us. Even with my eyes closed, I could see colors and light swirling around us. I felt light as if I was being lifted. It was exhilarating, sensual, and arousing. I felt lost in it, barely aware he was still there but still vaguely sensing his presence.

"Marjorie," he whispered. I opened my eyes. My hands were clasping his, but I was floating above him. Lights were weaving in and out, surrounding me, threading me to him. I was unsure of how to get down. He closed his eyes again, and the threads between us shortened, pulling me closer to him again. I closed my eyes again in acceptance, relaxing into his work until my feet were again on the floor. I opened my eyes again to see him standing there in front of me as he was before. The difference was that now we were both filled with magic and glowing. He pulled me in and kissed me deeply. He pushed me onto the bed as he slid on top of me, kissing me. The light was radiating from his body and encircling me as we joined our bodies. His lips met mine again, his hands caressing my body with the shimmering energies making it even more electrifying. The union of our bodies intensified the light. Bursts of light echoed peaks in my body. I'd never felt so close to anyone in my life, physically, emotionally, spiritually. We were one. As we reached our mutual climax, the lights brought us both up again—the room filled with a bright burst of light, lasting longer until we both collapsed together.

I heard applause in the hallway. Whether or not they'd been listening as Lazlo feared, that flash had to have been unmistakable, if that was normal for this type of union.

Lazlo rolled off of me, pulled me over to him, and held me in his arms as I rested my head on his chest.

"That was . . . amazing," I said as I looked up into his eyes.

He smiled. "As are you." We were both lost in each other. I slid my hand across his chest, circling my fingers in his chest hair.

"Would you like any refreshments, my love? I can request them if you like."

"Actually, yes, that would be lovely. I'd love some tea or a few crackers or whatever you have."

Lazlo slid out of bed. I watched him walk across the room, admiring the beauty of his form. He cracked open the door.

"We require refreshments in here." He shouted down the hall to someone who was waiting. He turned back to me, offering silent speech. *"Spirits have overtaken my staff, so they aren't themselves. I wanted to make sure you knew that before one came in here."* He came back to bed. He wrapped his arms around me. Suddenly the door opened. Roland scooted a cart bearing refreshments into the room. Lazlo broke away from me and rose out of bed, walking toward Roland and the spirit inhabiting his body.

"Thank you; we'll be fine from here," he said as he dismissed him, scooting the cart closer to the bed. "here you are, my dear," he said as he handed me a cup of tea.

"I know these aren't ideal circumstances. I know this isn't what you sought or how I wanted you to come to me, but no matter what happens next, I want you to know how happy I am that it was you who agreed to be my wife," he said.

The last part of that sentence still landed hard on me. That word was like a slap in the face. I'd lived my grown life hoping to avoid commitment because it always seemed to lead to disappointment. Now, what did I have but someone to worry about, someone who was worrying about me. I had a family again. Lazlo was now my family, his sister was my family, and his terrifying mother was as well. My book, however, was only useable by those with a blood lineage or blood-bond. Now I shared that with Lazlo as his wife. We were blood-bonded.

The book contained spells for healing just about any affliction. There were spells to prolong life and spells to end it instantly. Ancient, powerful incantations that no one else in the magical world could access. If others knew what the possibilities were, the real power contained within, I'd never have a day of peace. This was part of why I had always thought if I married at all, it wouldn't be to a magical person; that way, the magic stayed hidden and was available for emergencies only.

Now here I was, married to a powerful mage. Lazlo may have downplayed his abilities and knowledge, but I had a good sense of his enormous strengths after bonding with him spiritually and physically.

Family News

"Are you two finally done?" The voice from in the dark corner of the room startled both of us.

"Enough with the lovey stuff Lazlo. We've got work to do. Don't worry; no one can hear me but you guys. I'm a ghost to the ghosts." Ana stepped into the light, holding a finger aloft and pointing to her ring. "No magic can detect me, and I created an undetectable void in this room so we can talk as well."

"How long have you been there?" Lazlo asked with hesitation.

"You might have warned us," I said. I pulled up the covers to hide myself. Her intrusion felt weird.

"Don't worry; I was still outside when your light show went off. That's how I figured out where you guys were. Nice fireworks, by the way. Married, huh?"

Lazlo looked at me and smiled at that comment before he turned to Ana.

"So, Ana, what have you been able to learn so far, if anything?"

"Well, my intel so far is that the spirits are keeping inside the building. Occasionally one wanders to the grounds, but they don't seem to want to go anywhere, at least that's what I can see since I don't see any of them testing any boundaries. Your mother seems to have locked herself in the laboratory, so it is anyone's guess what she's doing in there."

"Nothing good, that much is certain. The possession is weaving into her, and she doesn't seem particularly stable." Lazlo commented.

Ana nodded. "Since we don't have enough intel yet, I'll leave you two lovebirds and do some more scouting. I'll check in with you again when I can, but the dampener leaves when I do, so watch your speech. I can confirm they are listening, although not intently. Just be careful." With that, Ana slipped back into the shadows.

Lazlo turned to me. "We'd best get some sleep now, my love. At least I know I need some." he grinned as he stroked my hair and kissed my forehead. The energetic exchange seemed more tiring than regular sex, and as much as I would have liked another round, I agreed.

He pulled me in close, holding me to his chest, and I returned the embrace. It felt as if the world was safe and secure when I was in his arms. We both quickly drifted off into sleep despite the worries and uncertainties of our current situation. We knew they should be satisfied that our marriage was sealed and official. That part seemed essential to Maeve, but neither of us knew exactly why or what her plan was.

In the night, I heard a voice. It was dark and haunting. "Fae kind, are only good drained and dead, I hate them. Do you know what I hate even more than those damn Fae? Huh? This fucking family. They have become weak and pathetic, and I will destroy them."

It was terrifying, so evil, so full of hatred. It was inside my head, or was it in a dream? I sat up with a start, my heart racing.

The room was dark. Lazlo was asleep by my side. I snuggled closer to him for comfort and managed to fall back to sleep.

******

We awoke to a loud bell with a servant I'd not seen before standing in the doorway. Both of us were startled by the loud clang and shouting,

"Breakfast is being served in the main dining room. The Lady of Ealach insists that you join her."

Lazlo spoke up. "I was rather hoping to get breakfast in bed with my new wife, but if Mother is calling, then we will answer the call to see what it is that she needs. Inform her that we will be down shortly." With that, the gentleman bowed at the waist and departed, closing the door behind him.

"What do you suppose that is all about? She was in such a rush to get us married you'd think we'd at least be allowed to be alone this morning."

Lazlo shrugged. "We won't know until we go downstairs. Hopefully, this will be brief."

I slid my hand down his naked chest. My body was hot to have him again, feeling as if that magical union was bringing parts of me back to life.

"I suppose she won't want to wait long enough for us to have a morning encore, will she?" I said, kissing his shoulder.

His hand gently met mine before it got below his waist. He lifted it and kissed my fingers.

"As much as that is a beautiful idea, no, she won't wait. If we start, we'll be interrupted. I don't think either of us wishes that."

"Absolutely not!" I said louder than I had intended.

The idea was somewhat horrifying. Ana popping out of the shadows last night had been bad enough.

We made our way into the dining hall to see her sitting at the head of the table. She stood as we entered the room and clasped her hands together.

"Ah, there you are. How pleasant to see your bright shining faces. I wanted to bring you up to speed on the news of my own life. The King will be here shortly to oversee our official transfer of power. All of my ties to this physical estate will be passed on to you two, and I will be free to continue my life without them."

"So Mother, if this has been an ongoing issue, why wait until now to attempt to resolve it? " Lazlo asked.

I noticed neither Maeve nor Lazlo mentioned Gwen at all. I assumed Lazlo omitted that to avoid any memory or attention being called to his sister.

"Lazlo darling, it wasn't an issue until you foolishly left this place unattended, and it called me back. It requires me to give up some powers I'd prefer to keep, but it will be worth it. My husband was none too thrilled that I rushed off to be here, of course, but the manor gave me no choice."

"So by your husband, I'm assuming you don't mean my father?"

"Oh no, he's long gone. He disappeared after I'd tried to kill him, silly man. But don't worry dear, he won't come home. I turned him into a wolf first. No, my husband is King Ceffert. I am officially your Queen."

She lifted her head with pride and managed to stand just a bit taller. This was an enormous accomplishment that she was pleased about.

"Once he arrives, refer to me as Your Majesty instead of Mother - unless one of us permits either of you otherwise. For now, please return to your room and make yourselves ready for a royal visit. Not those bedroom clothes you have on now, something nicer. You can return to your newlywed frolicking once we have departed." With that, she waved us out.

As weird as all of this was, I was relieved that she had indicated her plan to leave. Her absence would allow us to work on a plan to re-set things. A plan that would enable Lazlo and me the opportunity to live our own lives as we wished, rather than being tied to this place. Lazlo's grip tightened on my hand as we headed down the hallway in silence. The thought that his father might still be alive even if he was no longer human was news Lazlo must be glad to hear.

A Royal Visit

We made our way back up to Lazlo's bedroom, or our bedroom now. Roland was there hanging some garments that had been chosen for us for the state occasion. He bowed and walked out of the room, leaving the two of us alone again. The dress I'd been gifted was an exotic teal blue gown, it looked lovely hanging there, but how I'd pull it off, I wasn't sure.

Lazlo's garments looked regal, fitting of a Lord, echoing a similar color scheme as the gown. I had no doubt he would look amazing in them. I wondered where Ana was hiding. Would she pop out as soon as we got undressed? She seemed to have an odd habit of appearing suddenly. Her appearance when we were naked in bed had been unsettling.

Lazlo turned to me and sent a silent message. *"With Mother gone, we'll have more freedom. The libraries and studies and a laboratory are safe. I noticed Mother casting spells to keep the spirits out. I'm guessing she didn't want them overlooking any research she was doing. We'll be able to go there for privacy, but we'll have to pretend that isn't our intent, so it will need to be your idea as you aren't likely to know any of this yourself."* That was a relief to hear, a place to go away from prying ears.

The gown was a challenge to fasten, so Lazlo helped me get

into it as I didn't want to call anyone else. As anticipated, he looked magnificent.

I looked at him as he stood up after helping me straighten the skirt of my gown.

"You look amazing. I can't believe you're my husband." I paused for a moment as the words settled. "That feels and sounds so odd."

What was the oddest to me was that I minded it less. I didn't feel trapped with Lazlo as I had feared I would.

"My beautiful wife, you are stunning. True, it feels and sounds odd, but it is new, and for your part, this wasn't what you thought you were going to end up doing when I first invited you here. While it was on my mind, it was not what you were seeking."

Looking at him at that moment, I regretted nothing. I'd chosen well.

"Well, I suppose I'm as ready as I'll ever be. I've never met a King before. Have you?"

"Yes, more than one. This one, King Ceffert and his former wife came to our annual Midwinter celebration once or twice."

We reached the top of the stairs. A servant in a uniform that differed from that of those who worked here at the manor greeted us. There was a large group of people gathered downstairs already.

"I present Lazlo and Marjorie DuLaene," he declared before we were allowed to descend the staircase. The gathered crowd applauded. At that moment, I realized this was the first time I'd heard his surname, and suddenly without my consent, it was assumed it was now my surname. Odd. So much for choosing whether or not to take my husband's name. Maeve was outside the front door, and a carriage was pulling up. As we joined the crowd, we were continually congratulated on our recent nuptials. Several women gave me somewhat disappointed and judgmental energies through their fake smiles.

Suddenly a trumpet sounded. Everyone stood still.

The announcer declared, "KING CEFFERT AND QUEEN MAEVE."

They glided in together. The King had an air about him every bit as proud and self-righteous as I'd seen in Maeve. They were both drinking in the attention that came with their rank. He was not nearly as impressive in the looks department as she, but he was a generally handsome man with an undeniable charismatic aura. I could tell he was a mage himself by the ring on his hand, but the magic I sensed indicated he held power due to bloodline rather than innate abilities. Maeve, on the other hand, radiated immense power. Prior to her possession, I suspected she was already a formidable mage. With that added, she was more powerful than anyone I'd witnessed before. It was frightening to be in her presence, especially knowing that she was relatively unstable mentally. They moved to a makeshift throne where the King went to seat himself. Maeve seated herself at the smaller throne by his side.

"Now, where are that son and brand new daughter-in-law of ours, my Queen?" The King asked as he took his seat.

"There they are, my love," she pointed to us and beckoned us over.

We approached as requested. Lazlo bowed, and I managed a curtsey.

"What a handsome couple you are! I can see why your mother is so pleased with this match."

"Thank you, Your Highness," Lazlo said.

"I was quite sad to hear of the loss of your father. He served me well, as have you. I understand from your mother the responsibilities we are bestowing upon you will prevent you from joining us in any new campaigns. Pity. I've heard you've become quite the skilled swordsman." the King said.

"Your compliment is most gracious. It is always my aim to serve well, Your Highness."

"Well then, if the unrest continues, I may have need of your skills as a trainer for new officers."

"It would be my honor, Your Highness."

The King went on to detail his ideas for how Lazlo could accomplish this, what he wanted Lazlo to do. I stood quietly by Lazlo's side as he spoke. I knew nothing of this King or their customs here. None of that had resurfaced in my memories. Following Lazlo's lead seemed the best course of action.

Maeve sat by the King's side, remaining composed and looking radiant. A smile was creeping across her face, but she said nothing. She caught my eye. She was looking at me but through me. I heard the voice again. "Fuck you, Fae bitches." Which was followed by a burst of eerie laughter. I shook it off.

"Well then, enough of plans for the future. We'd best get ready to do what we are here to do and proclaim your official titles," the King said.

It made sense that this transfer had to be initiated by a mage of such rank. This was the transfer of power, the estate holder's title. It would unlock magics previously unavailable to Lazlo. I reached out to touch his hand. He locked his with mine. It helped sweep away the fear of that unsettling voice.

We took our leave of the King and Queen and were ushered into an adjoining room. We stood silently next to each other. Lazlo was offering no insight, and I had no idea what to expect.

I could only imagine what must be going on inside his head with all of these new revelations coming to light. This was a lot for anyone to take in. The simpler part for me was that none of this family drama was mine except by my marriage to Lazlo, so I had no heart in it; these people were strangers to me.

It wasn't long in that silence until an attendant came in and ushered us to our positions. We were directed to walk up the aisle toward the King and Queen, who were seated at the front of the assembly. There were a few whispers from the crowd as we passed, but all were silenced once we stood directly before the King and Queen. The two of them stood. I followed Lazlo's lead as he knelt

The King's voice filled the room. "I hereby proclaim Lazlo DuLaene the Lord and Master of this estate of Ealach, and all the possessions, powers, and responsibilities that come with it are now duly assigned to him. His mother, Queen Maeve, has relinquished her claims on this manor to belong solely to her son and his new wife. I also proclaim that Marjorie DuLaene, wife of this Master and Lord, holds the title of Lady and Mistress of Ealach as well as all powers and responsibilities that come with that assignment. Any heirs produced from this union have my blessing as well. Congratulations again to you both, and may you find many blessings in your life ahead."

With that, he tapped Lazlo on the shoulder with his scepter. A blue light emanated from it and flowed into Lazlo's body. As he stood, he was glowing. Maeve, I mean the Queen, approached me with a different scepter. I bowed my head as he had and felt violet light flooding me and surrounding me. Maeve then signaled me to rise and stand before them both.

"Join your lights," the King commanded. Lazlo took my

hands.

Suddenly the lights surrounding us flowed through our hands, and between us was a vivid indigo glow. It was quite a different feeling than the energy from the night before.

"What is mine is yours," Lazlo declared.

"What is mine is yours," I replied, praying that was the correct thing to say. It must have been as everyone seemed pleased, and as the King and Queen began applauding, the rest of the onlookers did the same. As I looked out onto the crowd of onlookers, I noted to myself it seemed there were many layers to these types of unions. I wondered why Gran never mentioned anything of magical unions in all the things she taught me. Perhaps she figured that I'd end up with a non-magical partner like most of my other ancestors. Then again, it seemed she had agreed to this marriage and alerted Lazlo to my whereabouts. Perhaps this had been what she wanted or thought I'd want.

Lazlo guided me down the aisle, away from the Royal pair, and back into the room where we had started. "That went well," he said as he turned to me. "I should have instructed you. I missed the opportunity. You followed well."

"What did all of that mean? What was with the light show?" My hands were trembling. The reality was setting in. I was becoming more frightened of what this all meant for me, for my life. "What was just transferred to me?"

Lazlo took my hands in his; the warmth was soothing. "I promise you. I will clear everything up. Right now, we still have to complete this Royal visit and bid farewell to my mother."

As if on cue, the doors flew open. Maeve and the King were standing in the entryway. Maeve approached us. "Well, Lord

DuLaene, it has been so wonderful all this catching up, and to finally get you married off was another huge accomplishment. I'll be back to check in, but for now, I've my things to do, laws to lord over, people to rule, the usual. Oh, and Lady Marjorie, keep him happy," she bent over and whispered in my ear, "I suggest lots and lots of sex. I'm sensing he's a bit bottled up in that department. My son is a romantic, but his adult sexual energy is off the charts. All the women here feel it."

A deep voice invaded my head. "Fuck him, Fae bitch," the voice was certainly not hers. Maeve then smiled and turned to the door where the King was waiting, offering her his arm, and they departed together out the front door. I was still stunned. These voices I kept hearing were unsettling. I wondered if I was hearing the spirit inhabiting her. If so, it was a terrifying and evil one, indeed.

Other unknown individuals who'd been in attendance were stopping to shake our hands and introduce themselves. Most of the attendees seemed to be residents of the town at the bottom of the hill, a few others had come from the King's court. They trickled out slowly until none were left but myself, Lazlo, and his usual, although currently possessed, staff. We both knew that Maeve had set things up to keep an eye on us. I suspected that she wanted to see what, if anything, we uncovered.

Experimentation

"Well, now that all of that is over, what's your desire, dear wife?"

Slipping into an area where we could work in private to uncover a solution to getting that spirit out of Maeve and the gate sealed seemed like the obvious choice.

"Well, my Lord," I said while sliding up close to him. "I think I want you to take me to the library over there and tear this gown off of me and have your way with me."

Lazlo smiled broadly. "My Lady, your wish is my command."

He pulled me in and kissed me while also pulling me over to the library door. He pushed me up against the door, making a show of kissing me and grinding his hips against mine before pushing the door open and allowing me to stumble into the room while the door closed solidly behind us. Once inside, he moved toward me again. This time I held out my hand to halt his advance.

"You have some explaining to do before we pursue this."

He seemed uncomfortable with the cease and desist order. I could see that the bottled-up comment held some truth and might have something to do with this new energy transfer.

He sat down in a nearby chair. "Very well. I am yours. Ask what's on your mind."

"What was unlocked? Do you even know?"

"In part. We've been handed some powerful tools. The frightening part is that Mother wouldn't have so willingly handed them over if she couldn't combat them, or there wasn't something far more valuable to her to gain by giving them to us," he said.

He was already looking restless in that chair.

"It could be something she hopes we open, or it could be something that the King has that she needs the freedom to pursue. You see, the spirit inside of her was also set free, no longer having any bind to this place or being called back just as she is now free."

I felt cold inside at that thought. Those voices I'd heard were unsettling. I wanted to know more before alarming him, unsure if he'd accept it as the truth or fear his new wife was losing her mind.

"As for me, I now have more control over the spirits. They have to listen to me. If desired, I also can tap into their energy directly. I didn't have that ability before. It was Mother's alone."

"So we don't have to worry so much about the spirits here now?"

"Not as much, but I suspect Mother has a pact with several of them that they will honor. We need to play along for now and use opportunities to see what we can access without them knowing much of anything. Our new abilities will require experimentation," there was a sly grin appearing on his face. "Please let me know when we are done with the line of questioning, and I can rip that lovely dress off of your body." his eyes were fixed on me intently, I could see his energy was expanding and needed a release.

"No," I said

He looked at me through a furrowed brow, clearly confused and not at all happy to hear that word.

"What do you mean by that?"

An aura of power was building stronger around him. Magics were forming that he seemed unaware he was commanding.

"I mean, I don't want you to rip this dress or tear it or even unbutton it."

"Okay. . .so I'm having sex with you while you are still wearing it?" He rose and approached me with intent in his eyes. Okay, that idea was also hot.

I backed away. "No, I want you to take it off of me without using your hands. I'm betting you can do that, and I want to see it happen. Don't make it disappear, though; that would be too easy."

Lazlo smiled and circled me. "Challenge accepted, and when I succeed?"

"I give myself to you in any way that you like, no questions asked."

He was enjoying this game I was playing.

"Are you sure, Marjorie, that this is a can of worms you wish to open? Me being truly able to undress you with my eyes?"

I laughed, suddenly aroused at that thought. "Well, we need to start figuring out what powers we do have, and it might as well be fun, don't you think?"

"Oh, what fun I have planned for you," he growled, looking at me with lust-filled eyes.

I felt the lacing in the back loosen as he continued to smile. There was zero hesitation. He had perfect confidence in his ability, even though this was something he'd never tried before. An invisible force was sliding buttons open, and the skirt fell to the floor as the top opened up and exposed my breasts as it slid to the floor along with the skirt. I was topless in a corset and some panties. I felt the corset's lacings begin to loosen until the corset fell over my hips and to the floor. He was taking his time now. I was standing there in only a pair of panties so completely turned on by the way he had slowly undressed me. He was still circling me, not touching me but closing in. He was close enough to feel his heat, his energy feeding into me.

"So do I have to melt the panties too, or have I passed your test?" He whispered seductively in my ear.

My knees felt weak at this point. "Oh, I think they are already melted." I managed to squeak out.

"Then you remove them yourself without your hands."

I pushed aside the initial "I can't do that" thought, and sure enough, I was easily able to command them down, and I stepped out of them, now fully naked. Lazlo had already also removed his shirt while he watched me lower the panties.

"Excellent job," he nodded in approval while I squirmed uncomfortably, unsure what he was going to ask of me next.

"Now what?" I inquired, rather uncomfortable just standing there while he stared at me, silent. It felt like an eternity before he spoke again.

"You truly do not realize how beautiful you are, do you?" He moved toward me, wrapping his arms around me. He began swaying back and forth. I could hear soft music echoing in the room. "Marjorie, you are something so special, so unique. I'm a lucky man."

He stopped swaying and kissed me before lifting me in his arms and carrying me over to a nearby couch, waving his hand as he lay me down and expanding the soft surface to a more suitable size for his plans. I could tell he connected to something by how he rolled his neck, and suddenly the light began again. There were different aspects to it this time, but it was still intense, still bright, although now we both had more color, and as we enjoyed our newlywed bliss, the light show surrounding us was spectacular.

Afterwards, as we lay together recovering our breath, I rested my head on his chest. I realized I felt content to be here with him. Still, a part of me longed to be free from all these curses and the bondage of my book. Now I was bound to him and his responsibilities as well. It was terrifying but also amazing when I looked at him as he held me in his arms. I wished my grandmother had been here to advise me.

I'd agreed to the marriage in haste, hoping for a plan to overcome what we both knew was a threat not only to us but potentially many others. Knowing now not only the magical, but political power she wields was an additional layer of terror, and I was glad I'd made a choice to join with him; losing him seemed too great a price to pay.

"Well, we'd best leave this room and venture where they expect us to be before they get suspicious, don't you think?" Lazlo said interrupting my thoughts.

I nodded and began to pick up the pieces of my gown and put myself back together. Suddenly I remembered another thing on my mind earlier. "Lazlo, how far have you ever been from this estate? What do you know of other, say slightly parallel worlds?"

"You mean where you were living as opposed to here? I honestly forget about that, but yes, I'm aware of other realms. I wasn't aware you were in one this entire time, but I'm aware of their existence." He pointed at the corset I had forgotten to put back on. "Carrying that might be a nice touch," he said.

"True, we don't want to look too put together, do we?"

"Certainly not. We want them reporting back that we can't get enough of each other. Which I hope there is some truth in," he said as his hand cupped my backside, and he pulled me into him.

"Much truth," I said grinding my hips against his, "I know I look forward to finding out what other magics we can wield to accent our exploration of each other."

He grinned mischievously. "I have a few ideas already."

My eyes widened. "Like what?"

"Oh, you will have to wait and see. The plans I have for you . . . For now, let's move on. They'll be wanting to serve dinner before long. Afterwards, we can sneak into another safe spot. This time, we will have more time since they won't be looking for us, and we can pull out some books in addition to exploring our new powers."

I was intrigued by his suggestion and very curious as to what was on his mind.

As we headed for the door, a familiar form greeted us.

"Geez, you two really need to keep your clothes on for more than five minutes if you want me not to show up and catch you naked."

In all the excitement, I think Ana has slipped both of our minds.

"Interesting ceremony. I thought they'd never leave, then they finally did, and you two had to get all hot and bothered again." Ana rolled her eyes.

"In all fairness Ana you did manage to interrupt our wedding night, as I recall. You can hardly blame us for needing more time together," Lazlo said, a little sternly.

"Lazlo, you've been locked up here too long. I'll give you

that. But c'mon man, an evil spirit possessing a questionable sorceress who is married to a King. I mean, this is potentially the fate of the world stuff so much bigger than, well, anything in your or anyone else's pants."

A twinge of discomfort came over me; her familiarity with him, the way she talked to him bothered me at times. Was this jealousy I was feeling? But she'd said evil spirit. Did she hear the voice also?

"What have you been able to find out from your searches?" Lazlo asked.

"Most of the spirits aren't happy being summoned. A few seem to be working with your mother, mostly the ones she installed in your staff, though." Ana's eyes darted around the room, assessing the area.

"Those are first on my agenda to rip out and send back," Lazlo said.

Ana nodded. " There are also members of the Collectors cult around. You know, that group of evil mages that seek ultimate power in objects and other magical beings. I haven't seen any on the grounds, but sense them somewhere."

"Ana, you mentioned an evil spirit. Do you have any further information about that spirit?" I asked.

"Not really, no. Just a sense that spirit means great harm to other beings and especially to this family, both Lazlo here and those poor trapped souls behind the gate. I sensed an intense hatred of these walls. The other spirits are afraid of it."

Lazlo looked surprised. "How did you get that? That's slightly more than I was able to get out of them, and they're supposed to talk to me."

"Only a feeling Lazlo. I can sense fear and hatred fairly easily. Gifts of my training and the Goddess. The ones working for your mother are either loyal to her or terrified of that spirit or a combination of both. That's all I can tell you. I don't suppose either of you read any of the books in here, did you? Nope too busy getting naked." She rolled her eyes again and sighed as she casually flipped a knife in her hand and allowed it to stick into the tabletop.

"So based on your assessment of the spirits, it seems I'm fairly safe to send most of them back. I mean, it sounds as if Mother primarily got what she wanted already."

"Well, the way you two are going at it, she may have even more sooner than expected. Geez, guys. If I don't know where you are off to, all I have to do is look for a light show."

"Ana, I think I speak for both of us in that we truly appreciate you not interrupting or letting us know if you arrived at an inappropriate moment."

"AHHH MY EYES" Ana screamed, staggered backward, and then broke into laughter.

Lazlo picked up a book and threw it at her. It flew through the air with significant force and speed. Ana dodged it effortlessly, and it hit the wall. Lazlo threw another one. She caught it and threw it back at him. In seconds the air was filled with things being flung in each direction. Ana and Lazlo were both dodging or blocking and countering. They were laughing. It was a game to them.

The sounds turned into a hum. I felt darkness surrounding me. A chill invaded my body as terror gripped my heart. I could hear that laughter, the sinister laughter I'd heard before. My head started spinning. The men at the cabin flashed in my head. There was someone else I could feel, another young woman. She was terrified. He was hurting her. I felt all her pain, all my pain. I could feel her anguish, her horror, the fear spilling out into her screams, my screams. I could hear them now, coming out of my body. I felt tears welling up and beginning to stream down my face. I withdrew, slumping to the floor and curling into a ball. Please let it stop.

Suddenly the room became silent, and I felt hands on my shoulders. "Marjorie. Marjorie, I'm here. It's alright." Lazlo's voice brought me back from that horrible place. I fell into his arms, sobbing. Ana stood aside. I sensed her watching, assessing me.

"I was afraid this would resurface. You've been through so much." He said as he was soothing me.

"No, it isn't that. Well, some, but it's more. I see things, terrible things, terrifying things, but it isn't all me. It isn't all mine."

Looking over at him, it seemed odd to see this broad man sitting on the floor next to me. I felt so small next to him. He stroked my hair, his fingers catching on a few strands.

"Do you want to talk about it? It could be the new magics you've inherited. They are ancestral. You could be tuning into a tragedy one of your ancestors suffered. But also your own trauma. Simply know that no matter what it is, I'm here," he said. I nodded.

He looked up at Ana. "Do you need anything? They'll be expecting the two of us for dinner shortly. If you need something, we can find a way to bring it to you."

She laughed. "I'm fine, Lazlo. As I said, I'm a ghost to the ghosts. I can get anything I need without detection."

Lazlo turned to me. "Are you alright to go back upstairs and change again?"

Ana was shaking her head. "I've never understood this changing clothes all the time thing you uppity types do."

Lazlo shrugged. "Come to think of it, I don't understand it either. It's simply what I've always done." He extended his hand to me and assisted me to my feet, keeping me close as we exited the library.

A Message from Beyond

After dinner, we headed into one of the studies that Lazlo pointed out. No ruse necessary; the spirits didn't seem to care. I wondered if our public displays of affection had embarrassed a few of them in some odd way.

"Your grandmother spent quite of bit of time in this study when she visited. I brought you in here thinking there might be something we could use; something that held her attention has to be noteworthy." Lazlo stood and wandered to one of the bookshelves and began looking over the selections. This new energy was changing him; he was more relaxed, more in control. Suddenly something occurred to me.

"Energy, we can follow the energy. There, that one. It has Gran's energy all over it." I could see it now. It glowed of Gran. This was part of what it meant for me to have my ancestral connections.

We spent the next while compiling books kept in that room that I identified as ones that Gran had been studying. One practically threw itself into Lazlo's hands. It was odd, red and blue with gold trim, and it was flickering between the two colors as he held it. He opened the book, and it floated in the air, out of his hands, just hanging there.

Aside from my grandmother's tag, the energy radiating from

it was ancient, unlike anything I'd ever seen. It was as if the book itself was declining to be touched but willing to make itself available to Lazlo.

We both stood and studied this phenomenon. Lazlo looked at me and then back to the book as if he suddenly had received some information. Then he closed his eyes, and white energy began to glow around him. As it swirled around him, small lights within the field circled his head, and then he traced some symbols in the air.

He opened his eyes but still looked distant, as if he was inside of something, perhaps the book itself. He seemed locked in communication. I witnessed a back and forth exchange. The response symbols were fast and furious, feeling like someone was frantically replying to his inquiry, desperate to reveal information. Suddenly Lazlo twisted my direction, flung out a hand, and a beam of multi-colored lights shot toward me. He turned back inward immediately as if he'd simply tossed something in my direction. As the light stopped in front of me, it began to take shape. The shape wasn't precise, but the energy was unmistakable. It came from my grandmother, perhaps a message hidden inside that book.

The eerie light beamed with a soft human-like energy. "My dear Marjorie, If you are seeing this, it means I'm gone, you've managed to make your way to Ealach and are reacquainting yourself with Lazlo. I knew I could trust him to get this to you."

I looked over at Lazlo. Gran had trusted him. I wondered even more why she had kept us apart.

"There is much I want to tell you, so much I kept from you out of necessity, so for that, I apologize. The truths you will need to uncover for yourself are too deep for this message, I fear, but you will find them on your own and at your perfect time. When Maeve reappears, be extremely cautious. She has a thirst for power and has accumulated much of it even before joining forces with her ancestral spirit. Her magic is dark, powerful and hungry. Much inside you she craves, so be cautious, tread carefully when you learn your powers. Hide as much as possible from her."

Once again a vague reference. Even Gran wouldn't spell things out for me.

"Lazlo is a good man. I apologize for not allowing you to remember him or our agreement with his family or, more recently, tell you of mine with him. Trust that my reasons were sound. If you'd remembered, you would have made your way here far too soon and been at risk. Even Lazlo couldn't have saved you, and he may have perished himself. You are both much stronger today, but still in great danger if you do not heed my warnings."

With that, the light dimmed, and my attention went back to Lazlo. He was clearly in conversation with someone or something amid lights flowing all around him. He was smiling, laughing as they circled him. There were shapes, long slender, some small, and one enormous one curled up in front of him. It looked like some type of a dragon, although I thought they were only mythological beings. And yet there was one, plain as day, curled up on the floor and conversing with my husband. Husband. Even in my mind, that was still a strange concept. It felt so odd to think of myself as joined to anyone. There was still so much I didn't know about this man. Did he know there were dragons in this book he grabbed? Had he talked to these creatures before?

He seemed utterly lost in there, not in a harmful or dangerous way, simply that he was immersed and seemed to be enjoying himself. I was enjoying watching as I'd not seen him quite like this before. I admired his spirit, his look, his confident demeanor. I stepped outside of myself to see how he might look to other women. What I saw was that they'd fall all over him, that I'd have to be the partner he needed, I'd have to be on my own A-game if I were to keep this man as happy and fulfilled as he deserved to be.

I stood there admiring him when he turned to me again. This time his eyes met mine, and his light invited me into the circle. The beam became an extension of his hand and he drew me in with him and his fascinating friend.

"I'd like you to meet Besekdlsa. Besekdlsa, this is my wife, as you are aware."

Lazlo's tongue had an unusual tone at the pronunciation of the name. It was as if he spoke it in a different language, and I attempted to interpret it with my limited knowledge. The dragon lifted its head, and the eyes of the beautiful creature examined me. His head turned back to Lazlo.

"Be cautious, protect her at all costs," he said to him before his head turned back to me."Lady Marjorie, it is indeed a pleasure to meet you."

The creature's head tilted down as if in a bow. He lifted his eyes back up to me. I offered a curtsy in return.

"There is much you are to learn, much many of us do not have the answers to, but inside you are tremendous resources of ancestral knowledge you may begin to tap into. Beware, however, because there are those who seek the energies within you. They will destroy you and all you love to obtain them. It was the price your dear mother paid."

I knew very little of my mother. My grandmother had told

me of her tragic death, that it was due to one of the legendary time-cursed books and that my father, her son, took his own life shortly afterwards. Other than telling me that she shared very little of their history.

She mentioned my father on occasion, but she preferred to focus on me, on bringing me up and teaching me the things she had learned to make sure our legacy continued. My father had been exceptionally talented in the alchemic arts, according to what she did tell me. Still, the mention of my mother, their love, courtship, and what life they had together, she glossed over, telling me nothing of who my mother was aside from being the love of her son's life.

I did find it odd that he'd have abandoned me after her death based on the things she said about him, but she never went into detail about his tragic end either. Gran's version was somewhat tidy. I'd suspected it wasn't as straightforward as she said for quite some time. I always thought it was her pain keeping her from telling me more, but now I wondered, even about those motives. Who was my mother?

The surprised look on my face at the dragon's mention of my mother seemed to have registered with him. The elegant head of the creature tilted.

"It didn't surprise me that Lord Lazlo knew nothing of your mother, but you appear not to know much of her either. Her powerful blood runs in your veins. That substance itself creates a power that others lust after and will attempt to destroy you to possess as they did her. There is much for you both to learn here; I will do my best to guide you and send others to assist you as well."

Lazlo bowed to the dragon.

"Thank you, Besekdlsa. Your assistance and support are

truly appreciated. We will, of course, do as instructed, and if there is anything that we can do to aid you and your brethren, we are ready to assist as well," he said.

The dragon nodded. "And we are here for you. Now that you have been fully connected with both sides of your heritage, you may call on us for aid. We can easily hear and answer, just as we do for your father."

The glow of red and blue shimmering all over the dragon's illuminated body was breathtaking. The pure power, strength, and sense of safety I felt were unlike any I'd encountered before.

Lazlo bowed and stepped back, pulling me beside him, and the circle collapsed as the book itself landed gracefully on the table.

When he turned to face me, I could sense something different in him. The colors in his eyes were shifting as if he was processing perhaps new energy? I wasn't sure what it was, but I felt confused and overwhelmed by all that had just transpired.

He shook his head, his beautiful hair swirling across his face, and then he seemed to have shaken it off, whatever it was going on inside that beautiful body of his.

"Wow, that was quite a thrill," were the first words out of his mouth. "A bit to recover from on my part, and I am guessing on yours as well. Are you alright, my love?" he asked as he traced a hand across my face.

I felt as if my body was going to explode, or my mind was completely frazzled. Suddenly I was shivering all over and fell into his arms and began sobbing. I didn't know why or what was coming over me, but I had no control over it. As he held me, I felt a warmth run through me, surrounding me. I could feel and hear his heartbeat, and it was such a soothing sound. He allowed me to wrap around him, and he enclosed me as well.

"I'm sorry," I managed in between sobs.

"Nothing to be sorry about; you've been through a lot in this short time. Know that I am here for you, that I am your lover, your protector, and your friend as well as your husband. I will never leave you, Marjorie. Not of my own free will."

I looked up at him from my head against his chest. "Is none of this weird for you?"

He smiled and kissed my forehead. "Oh, this? Floating books, new magic? Ghostly wedding? Crazy Mother? It's all weird. I invited you here in hopes of a reunion, certainly hoping to court you but admittedly not expecting to marry you so quickly."

One thing had been bothering me, something we had not as yet had a chance to discuss.

"The bloody children your mother had with her? What was that all about? I saw them as we came in. Their eyes followed me. They were covered in blood, and much of it appeared to be their own as if they were dead but not dead."

Lazlo was silent as he stroked my hair. I kept quiet, giving him time to process. Did he even want to answer? Was it too awful?

"The Collectors, that Ana mentioned earlier, they use children. The sect hunts Fae. Children can see or sense them the best, so those children are their hunters. The children were offered as sacrifices, stolen or runaways. Based on their presence when Mother arrived, I can only guess that she is part of that sect or somehow involved with them these days."

"Hunt Fae? Fairies?" The cruel words echoed in my mind,

and I shuttered. "Do they even exist? I thought they were extinct?"

"They are exceedingly rare or hide extremely well. The healers we met in the wood were Fae or very connected to them. I'm uncertain as they never revealed to me their part in this or who they were exactly. There was a time when some magicians learned how to cultivate their magic by harvesting their blood and certain parts, the fairies being the most sought after."

The words of the man at the cabin rang in my head. "The ones they don't grind up, that is," I shuddered at the memory.

"Most magicians won't touch anything so dark and dire but those that hunger for power unfortunately still do. Many theorize that the Fae opened several portals to other realms where most of them are living happily. I'd certainly like to believe that, although some may move back and forth. It's difficult to know since it often leads to their death once they are revealed."

"The more I learn, the more it feels like I have to learn. I grew up in a very different place. I thought most spells had herbs in them, and I never conversed with dragons or any other beings of that sort."

"Perhaps you never actually conversed with them but trust me, they were with you. Your grandmother spoke of them; she was aware even if she never fully opened your eyes. I understand her reasoning for removing you from this realm with all its reliance on magic, far different than the technology you have spoken of, where you were living. There can be much danger here."

His hands were absently caressing me as he spoke. Once again, I found myself wishing I could remember my blocked memories. It was becoming clear I'd been Lazlo's first love and he'd never lost those feelings. I wondered what my feelings had been. All I had was a vague story about a guy named Lance that seemed more about sex than an actual romance.

"Most magicians tend to stay in one place rather than travel a lot. Traveling mages tend to be seeking something, and often it isn't something that benefits anyone other than the mage. However, sometimes it's simply a quest for knowledge, but other magicians aren't kind to strangers, and non-magic users can be quite distrustful of us no matter how pure our intentions."

"I'm sorry, this is so much to take in. I came here to visit, but now I'm bound to you, and I assume to this realm?"

Lazlo shrugged. "To me, yes. To this realm, that depends. Of course, we need to work through these spells, but once we figure all of that out, we shall both be able to move more freely, and perhaps you can take me and show me where you were living. I'd love to see it".

He held me tighter, kissing the top of my head this time. The warmth of his embrace was comforting. When I'd left to come here, I was homeless. I'd just sold most of my belongings and given up the apartment, unsure where I was going next. This trip was supposed to be a quick detour before I devoted myself to a gypsy lifestyle. Everything I owned was in the bags I had brought with me to Ealach.

I snuggled my head against his chest. "I'd love to show you."

It was nice to have this tender moment with him. We stood like that, silent and holding, stroking each other as he comforted me, and I, in my way, was attempting to comfort him. After all, it hadn't been exactly easy for him either.

His hand slid down my back. He cupped my face with the

other hand and brought his lips to mine. The kiss was so tender and sweet. He pulled away. As we looked at each other, we felt our heat rising. I was ravenous for him. I kissed him back passionately, letting him know what I wanted. Together we worked to get each other undressed. "No magic, no lights, just you," I whispered.

"No lights, no Ana either," he replied with a smile.

We both needed the feel, the touch of each other, raw, animal lust. He lifted me in his arms, pushing me against the wall and lowering my body to join with his. His strength was exhilarating, the way he held me. I loved the feel of him inside of me, his groaning in my ear. I loved hearing him make that sound, knowing I was giving him that pleasure. We both needed that release, to feel each other so intimately.

After we were both satisfied, he lowered me to the study floor. He helped me to the ground, where I simply collapsed, and he lay down beside me. I started laughing. At first, he just looked at me; then, he started laughing as well. I grinned and slapped his chest with both of my hands.

He responded by tackling me. There we were, naked, rolling around on the floor, now laughing and playing. It was such a fantastic feeling. He stopped, having managed to pin me beneath him.

"I am the luckiest man in the world to have such a wonderful woman." He looked at me with such love in his eyes. I smiled back at him, still attempting to get my arms free from his grip.

"Well, you tell that wonderful woman that you belong to me now, and she can't have you!" He looked at me quizzically.

"You are an odd one, but I do love you. I think I'm the one that has *you*, since currently, you're the one pinned down. So you'd best give up the fight."

I slid my legs up against his chest in an attempt to break free of him, but I couldn't unseat him. I'd have to admit he'd won.

"Okay, you win, but it's hardly fair; you're much bigger than I am."

"Ah, but you're smaller and faster, so you have potential."

"So what did you win since we never set terms ahead of time?"

"Well, since you were the one you started it, I think that I won two things as I see it. First is I get to carry you upstairs and put you to bed. I think you need rest to process. The second is that I get to train you. You need to learn how to fight. I think our experiences outside have taught us the need for it, and I'll not lose you because you were unaware of a skill I could've easily taught you."

I sighed. "I was kind of hoping it would be a sex thing but okay."

"You're an incorrigible woman. Here let's get you back in this dress unless you want me to carry you naked through the halls. And don't think I wouldn't do that either if you don't behave."

"I kinda am liking this bossy you. It is pretty hot," I teased.

"And I adore sassy you," he said as he helped lace up the dress enough to keep me covered. "No sense in putting it on tightly since I'm only taking you to bed, and yes, Marjorie bed to sleep. I have a few things to attend to, and then I'll rejoin you, but you need rest even more than I do right now."

I knew he was referring to my earlier meltdowns. I was admittedly feeling somewhat frayed at the edges. Sleep would help.

I nodded. "Now that you mention it, yes, that does sound nice."

With that, he scooped me into his arms, and I went limp and closed my eyes, relaxing into him. I felt myself drifting into sleep as I could feel him carrying me up the stairs. I stirred as he laid me on the bed and undressed me. I attempted to help, but the sleep in my eyes was so heavy I could barely move. He tucked me into the bed and kissed my cheek. "I'll be back love, sleep well."

Strange Dreams

I stirred from my slumber when I felt the warmth of Lazlo crawling into bed next to me. He wrapped me in his arms, and I drifted back off to sleep.

In that slumber, I experienced a vivid and colorful dream. A man and a woman were running. I could feel fear, particularly in her. They sought shelter in a beautiful greenhouse. There was love between them. There was a loud thud on the roof, then a second thud. They looked up and there were two of the dead children, their eyes turned to the woman, fixed on her. She screamed but quietened quickly as the man helped her move out of their sight.

I felt her heartbreak at what had happened to these children, how horrified she was at this. They were working their way to the opposite end of the greenhouse quickly. The children were slow. They knew that but also were aware that reinforcement might be waiting for the children - the hunters on the other side.

The far side of the greenhouse door blew open. A long slender dragon head and neck came inside. "Hurry," it said. The couple rushed to it and its protection. Her heart was beating so fast. She was so terrified. He was steadfast with her, and the dragon had come to their aid. Still, she dared not think she was going to survive. She had been running for so long. Every bit of her emotions tore through me as though they were my own.

My heart must have been racing, or I must have been making some noise or movement because I felt Lazlo's arms tighten around me, his head pressed against mine as if to comfort me. My eyes opened and lifted my gaze to meet his.

"Are you alright? That must have been some dream you were having," he said softly.

"Yes, I'm fine; it was… odd. And frightening. But then again, I have a lot to process. Have you been awake long? What have I missed?" I asked.

I noticed he was dressed. Bright sunlight shone through the window. He'd let me sleep in quite a bit.

"Well, I brought you breakfast, so there's that. If you're hungry, that is." He moved the cart over to the bed to showcase what had been brought up for me.

"As for anything else, I've been doing some experimenting. I've created a safe bubble where we can discuss things without any of the spirits understanding or hearing what we are saying. They won't even realize there is any sort of interference, which is the best part of it. We can talk anywhere we want now, not just in those specific rooms or in Ana's presence," he said.

"Wow, almost actual privacy. That's a plus."

"Most certainly. I learned how to release my staff and have already done so. Mother has to expect it. That shouldn't raise any alarms. I consider them friends in addition to employees, and I couldn't allow this to continue."

"Are they alright? That had to be weird."

"Thankfully, none of them have put in notice. They've all been offered additional compensation as well. I feel terrible.

No one should be forced to endure what they were put through."

"What else have you discovered?" I asked.

"It seems Mother dismantled more of the gate protections than I'd realized. It'll take me more time to rebuild than I'd anticipated. However, once again, she has to expect that I will do that, and it should come as no surprise."

"Well, if it is, I suppose she would just pay us a visit herself, right?"

"Most likely. I'm still uncertain of her true motivation. She wanted to make sure that she wasn't called back here or bore any responsibility for this manor. Whatever power play she's crafting, that distance is necessary, and if her master plan will cause harm to others, many of the ancestral spirits here would try and stop her or slow her down considerably. Now they cannot touch her."

"I saw those hunter children in my dream. They were after a woman. I'm unsure if I was connecting with something real or it was my way of processing some of that information, but it felt real and was terrifying. I could feel her terror and her heartbreak at what had happened to those innocent souls."

I was still nervous to tell him about the voice I'd heard. I was more and more certain it was the spirit controlling his mother. It felt as if it was confronting me or my family lineage. Why he would hate us or want to destroy a family with only one living member was beyond me, but the threat was terrifying.

"I wish I knew where the Fae hunters figured in all of this. I knew Mother had meddled in darker magics but had no idea she was ever involved with them."

At that moment, I looked out the window, and my heart froze. Standing in the courtyard, staring up at the window were two children. They were too far away to see those terrifying eyes, but their heads were tilted upwards as if they were looking up at our bedroom.

"Lazlo!" I said, pointing at them. My heart was racing. What were they doing here? Who were they hunting? The memory of the screech and harshness of the pointed finger from my first encounter sent a cold shot through me. Did Maeve leave them here to watch us? Was there something about me that attracted them?

Lazlo walked through the door onto the balcony outside the window. He stretched out his arms and looked to the sky. Then he clenched his hands into fists and thrust them downward. A beam of light formed in front of the children, forming an energetic wall. We could no longer see them beyond that light. I wasn't sure whether they had vanished or whether they were simply obscured. Then he shot another beam of light out of his hand that traveled far beyond where I could see.

"I've reinforced the area. They can't come through. I also sent a message to Mother to tell her to get those filthy hunters off my grounds. I'm confident she'll remove them if she hasn't already recalled them. With what I have learned in these past twenty-four hours, I'm not afraid of her, not if she comes at me. Yes, she is powerful; but I can hold my own now that I am fully instated as Lord of this manor."

The confidence in his voice, and with the powerful magic I had just witnessed, assured me he was right in feeling that way. For myself, I was feeling somewhat inadequate. After all, I was a kitchen witch who relied primarily on herbs and recipes. I had other innate abilities, and spells I could cast, but nothing like what I'd just witnessed. This man I'd chosen to wed was quite powerful. And while power itself had never been anything I'd admired in another, it was comforting to see knowing that this was the man who'd sworn he would protect me.

"Was that something you learned last night while I was sleeping? Did you sleep at all last night?"

"I mentioned I'd been experimenting, and I found a time dilation spell, so truthfully I was up all night but then was able to step back several hours and still get some sleep. I was on a roll, so I didn't want to stop. Ana was helping me. It was quite productive."

Part of me was instantly envious of Ana. Not only did she know more about Lazlo than I did, but she'd gotten precious time with him that I missed because of my current lack of strength.

"Would I be correct in guessing that you led me to believe initially by the act of omission that you knew less to start with than you actually did?"

"I suppose that may be correct. I never said I was helpless, but your presence, well, perhaps that sidelined me a bit, and I wasn't showing as much of myself as I might have otherwise." He smiled and stroked my hair. Those eyes, how could I ever have forgotten them?

He leaned into me, almost whispering. "Now what's amazing to me, what I'm focusing on is that I find myself channeling dragon energy in addition to the ancestral magic. I was always able to channel a small portion of the ancestral magic, more after Gwen abdicated, and even more after Mother and the King declared me Lord of the manor. The dragon energy is brand new to me. It is as if that encounter yesterday unlocked something inside me. It's an amazing feeling."

So there it was. I'd married a man I barely knew and

was watching him change before my eyes. The annoyingly frightening part is that he was only getting sexier.

"So, how are you feeling this morning? Better rested, or do I need to tuck you back in to sleep some more before we begin your training? Ana is willing to share her knowledge as well. She seems very dedicated to keeping you safe."

I wrinkled my nose at him. "Can't you and I just wrestle naked after sex?"

Lazlo laughed."Of course we can, but I am serious about getting you to learn to take care of yourself when it isn't playing. I want you to learn how to fight standing up, how to use weapons - swords, knives, or any other of your choice. Magic can fail us at times, or we can be in a situation where it isn't the most appropriate defense, and we need to be prepared."

I sighed, a sense of defeat at not being able to avoid it. "I've slept well enough. What am I wearing for these lessons? Surely not one of these dresses you have had me parading around in."

I had very little interest in fighting. It was never a curiosity for me, and as badly as I felt I performed when faced with the necessity, I wasn't keen on going back into it. Play fighting was okay, but actual fighting? Well, most of my life, I'd avoided it.

Lazlo presented some sensible attire, comfortable pants, and a form-fitting shirt. Both moved with me, they weren't overly tight, but I could move freely, at least as far as I could tell.

"You'll want to make sure your hair is tied back properly. I'm heading downstairs. Meet me in the study, and I'll take you to the entrance to the laboratory and our training room."

The Whirling Warrior

I surveyed myself in the mirror to figure out how to best bind my hair for battle. Battle? My crazy chaotic hair had often been an issue, my version of a battle. I worked it into a somewhat messy braid. I never was very good at hairstyles, but I felt the need for something that might stay with this fighting stuff, and the braid seemed more sensible.

When I walked into the study, he had a sword in his hand, examining it. He had a few other weapons spread out on the table. Despite his build, I hadn't thought of Lazlo as the warrior type when we first met. After seeing him in action I knew he was downright impressive.

"You look well. Are you ready to begin?" Lazlo asked.

I wasn't sure how ready I was for whatever this was going to be. My brain started ticking and I wondered how easily he'd be distracted by sex. I found myself wishing I hadn't buttoned up my shirt all the way. Perhaps there would be an opportunity to change that. However, I had the feeling that Lazlo was on a mission and that even if I did distract him, that would only be a brief distraction, and who was I kidding? I was not getting out of this.

He motioned me to a door on the other side of the room. When we entered, the room was nothing more than an empty space with no windows.

"This is the practice room. You could also call it part of the laboratory as this is where we come to practice more defensive spells as well as physical fighting skills. The walls here will give if you end up throwing yourself against them."

He pointed to a door on the far left side of the room. There was a window in it as well that looked out into this room.

"That's the potions laboratory. You may have some memory of it?"

I shrugged. "Perhaps a vague sense. Gran was in there a lot when we were here, I think?"

"Quite true."

So this is where he'd been last night. There were memories just beyond reach, I knew I'd seen this before, but nothing more clear was coming.

"Ana, where are you hiding. I know you are in here. Show yourself and help Marjorie get prepared."

The room must have been larger than my initial impression because out of a shadowed area that I thought was just a wall, walked Ana.

Lazlo smiled at her, bowed, and left us alone. For the next several hours the two of us worked together. Ana was incredibly skilled, and I felt like a complete clod.

I was losing patience with myself. Thoughts of the men on the train surfaced, how helpless I'd felt. The thought distraction cost me. I didn't move and Ana's punch connected. It brought me back.

"I pulled that. If I hadn't, you'd be on the ground. You have to keep your mind clear," she said.

I nodded. My head was spinning. I was tired, frustrated, and longing to be elsewhere. Still, I knew I didn't want to end up with one of those gangs again. That thought motivated me. As much as I didn't like this, I had to do it.

We went a few more rounds before Lazlo came strolling back into the room. He watched for a while. When we stopped, he approached.

He looked at me. " Do you mind sitting out? You look as if you are doing well, but I'd like to borrow your trainer if you don't object."

"As long as she is okay with it?" I turned to Ana, who I could see was grinning.

Ana nodded. "I think a quick break might do you good," her eyes still on Lazlo.

"Then are you ready for a go with me?" Lazlo asked.

"Absolutely," she said.

Lazlo turned to me, giving me a quick kiss.

"Go into the laboratory. Watch at the window if you like or explore what is kept in there. You may find some things of interest." He lifted his sword and twirled it grinning at Ana. "Or prepare some remedies in case one of us gets the better of the other." He leveled his eyes at his opponent.

They immediately began circling each other. I hurried out of the way and went behind the door as he instructed. What followed was a flurry of swords, arms, and legs. Lazlo, despite his size, was quite fluid, even graceful. Ana was just as quick and fluid as he was. However, with her smaller, more slender physique, it was more expected. I couldn't tell what was going on, but they appeared to be even in skills. I could hear them even though I was in the other room. The banter between the two of them increased in intensity as they locked swords; each one was taunting the other. After what seemed like hours but was probably only minutes, Ana did a twirl with an extended leg. Lazlo didn't see it in time, and he fell hard onto the floor.

"HA!" Ana shouted. "Bigger they are, harder they fall, " she proclaimed as she pointed her sword at him.

Lazlo began to rise before she sheathed her sword and offered him a hand up. He nodded. "Good match. It appears you've learned a few new tricks. You certainly kept me on my toes. How about round two. See how you fare against magic."

Ana nodded in agreement, a sly smile across her face. It was clear they were both enjoying the sport of the exercise. Lazlo still had his sword, but this time it was cackling with blue electric energy. I had the feeling that was the new magic he had uncovered, which was why he was so keen on using it. This time Ana couldn't get close to touching him. Warrior to warrior, they were even, but warrior to warrior-mage, Ana was falling behind. Still, she was impressively holding her own, managing to defend herself against his attacks. He grazed her a few times, but mostly she managed to avoid any blows, sword, or magic. However, what had turned for her was the sheer impossibility to reach Lazlo with any of her attacks. She was purely in defensive mode. Oddly she didn't seem frustrated by it at all; she seemed to be enjoying the challenge, forever looking for a break as if she knew he would feel overly confident, or that mages usually did. Lazlo was up and down, experimenting with this new energy. He could float above her at any time but also wasn't as steady when he left the ground for more than the occasional leap.

Suddenly out of nowhere, Lazlo landed a solid blast. Ana recoiled, stumbled, and then started spinning, not doing anything else, just spinning. A vortex seemed to be pulling everything down. Light began to shine out of her, reaching to the ceiling and spreading across it. Lazlo was no longer able to maintain his magical flight and landed rather solidly on the ground. He attempted to counter, but the magic just bounced off of her whirling body. As she continued, I saw him begin to struggle as if he couldn't breathe. She was not stopping, nor did she seem to be aware of him or anything else. Lazlo was no longer able to stand, beginning to fall to his knees. Ana kept up her dance. Then he collapsed, unmoving on the floor. She was still whirling, light emanating from her.

'When I threw open the door the air rushed out toward her. "ANA STOP!"

I screamed at the top of my lungs. The sound echoed throughout the chamber, and Ana's dance halted instantly. She seemed to be realizing the damage she had been doing before her legs gave out, and she sunk to the floor.

When I arrived at Lazlo's side he was barely conscious. I held him and rubbed his chest and he began breathing more normally as the air in the room shifted now that Ana had let go of her magic. Magic was all I could think to call it. I certainly had never seen anything like it before. As soon as Lazlo was able, he reached for Ana.

"Ana, are you alright? I did not mean to hit you so hard. I am so sorry."

She nodded but said nothing, eyes still a bit glazed. Lazlo rose and motioned me over to her. "Stay with her a moment Marjorie. I'll be right back."

"Ana." I touched her shoulder. She looked at me, and tears were forming in her eyes.

"I could see her. She was so beautiful. She was lifting me up, joining with me. I've never felt so close before."

"Who, Ana?"

"The Goddess Oya. My Goddess. The one I serve. She

told me to come back, to stop, that it wasn't time, but I didn't want to stop. Then when you called to me, she threw me back herself, or I'd have kept going until she claimed me."

"And until you killed Lazlo and possibly myself, by the looks of it."

"Oya would never allow that. It was me in my foolishness that was blinded momentarily."

The sound of her voice was still a tone of one in complete awe.

I felt so alien. I didn't know the deities here, and I had no clue what this meant to her. Lazlo returned with a bottle of something he had collected in the other room.

"Here, Ana, this should replenish you. I thank you for being such a good sport when these energies are new to me, but I was wrong to risk you like that."

Ana chugged the contents of the bottle. "Whew, that brings me back down, damn. That's harsh stuff, Lazlo."

He smiled. "Indeed, it is. Yet it's effective."

Ana shook her head and pointed at Lazlo. "Whatever it is you're tapping to create that energy, I've never felt anything like it. I think that's why I flipped that switch, and then the energy I absorbed was so intense, I lost all sense of things."

"It's a good thing then that when we were working last night, I never directed anything at you. I think the more I use it, the stronger it's getting. As for you, I understand now why so few have seen a whirling warrior and lived."

Ana nodded. "Once that gets going, it's difficult to stop. That's why we spend so much time connecting to the Goddess. She intervened this time. She knew you weren't a threat and didn't deserve to die. She understood I was lost in a moment. Typically that move I threw is a suicide move as well. It would've killed all of us in this enclosed space."

Ana recognized the look of horror on my face. "Don't worry, now that I know what I'm dealing with, I'm better prepared. He caught me off guard." She turned to Lazlo. "I think we need to work with that energy, hitting me with it in lighter bursts, so I grow more accustomed to it and don't trigger again."

Lazlo shook his head. "Not until I've done more with it on my own and have better control over its intensity. I hit you with far greater force than intended. My control needs to be better, as well. Once I can demonstrate that level of control, I can help you build immunity but not until then. It's too dangerous," he said.

I was glad to hear he had that level of sensibility. As resistant as I had been to getting married, I had no desire to lose him.

"Alright, then. Traditional sparring only it is. I can live with that," Ana said.

"Well, for now, are you up to working with Marjorie some more? She had a good break, and seems to be making progress," he said.

"I'm good," Ana said.

"Excellent. I'll go see to my daily duties and meet up with you both later," Lazlo said.

He kissed me and walked out of the training room. I turned to face Ana.

"Alright, pixie girl. Front and center. Show me what you got." Ana commanded.

It was annoying that this was my only option with my diminished magic. Still, the longer we trained, the more I began hearing, sensing, and feeling things I hadn't been aware of before. Something seemed to be growing inside of me. I managed to tap into enough to counter a move and better Ana at one point. I knew I'd sensed what she was going to do next. I wasn't sure how but it gave me hope that more was returning to me.

After a while, Lazlo reappeared. "I've been successful in sending most of the ancestors back where they belong and making sure the ones remaining are friendly to us, not reporting to Mother. I don't doubt that this will eventually bring her back here." He turned to Ana. "If you can stay on a while, I'd like you to keep working with Marjorie on her combat skills. If not, we understand and appreciate all you have done for us."

Ana nodded. "Thanks. I'll meditate on it and see what my orders are. Then I'll let you know."

I felt bad that after all Ana had done for us, I wanted her to leave. The selfish part of me simply wanted time alone with Lazlo. Then again, we needed her here. We needed her help. Still, her belief was strong, and I knew she'd go where her Goddess and her Order instructed her to go.

A Quiet Evening

"Come, my love. We've much to do," Lazlo said as he extended his hand to me.

He looked back at Ana. "Will you be joining us for dinner? Now that the spirits are in line, we don't have to worry."

She smiled. "Thanks for the offer. I need to find a quiet space for the evening. Skipping dinner is better for me."

"Understood. We'll see you in the morning then."

I took Lazlo's hand and walked out of the practice room with him. He led me down the hallway and into a nearby library. He shut the door and turned to me.

"I sense something isn't right. Please talk to me. I can feel you. Now more than ever. What's going on inside that beautiful head of yours?" I sat down in a nearby chair and looked up at him.

"Truly, nothing is wrong. I'm only sorting out feelings, feelings I'm not used to having."

"I'm afraid I need more than that. I can't read your mind without you allowing it, but I can feel your feelings. The magical bond we share allows that. I feel you sure, yet unsure, and it's rather unsettling."

"Can you just tune it out while I sort myself out?"

He smiled. "I don't want to do that. If something needs to be addressed, please do so." He wouldn't let go of my eyes, holding them with his. I looked away.

"It's dumb, and I'm embarrassed to talk about it." I averted my eyes from his. "I feel selfish saying anything."

"I can't help you if you don't tell me," he said.

I took a deep breath. He was right.

"Well, I've kept people at a distance all my life. I never let anyone get too close. I've felt a longing for someone but what I feel with you is different than I've ever felt before." There I got that far. Discussing my feelings was never easy for me, not like this anyway.

Lazlo nodded. "We were thrust into this faster than either of us anticipated. I feel a certain amount of confusion myself, although my feelings for you have never been unclear." Again, the reminder of what I didn't know, the things I'd forgotten. It was an ache inside of me.

"I just . . .I want to be alone with you. No one else around. No staff, just us. I know it isn't practical with all that's going on, but especially after what happened today, I want you to myself for a while."

"Well, I won't argue with that sentiment," he said. He extended a hand to help me up from the chair.

"I think dinner in our bedroom might be what we need. I'll have Roland bring things up to us. I'll instruct him that we're not to be disturbed. I will, however, bring some books I found that I think we need to review. How does that sound?"

"It sounds perfect. I'm ready for dinner, those books, and time alone with you." I smiled.

Our evening alone was productive. The information we were absorbing about spirit possession and removal was helpful. Since these were spells that neither of us had done and there was no way to try them out, it was going to be risky.

Next was the spell to permanently dismantle the gate. It was no longer necessary to seal it temporarily. We knew where Maeve was. We also knew it was probable that it wouldn't be long before she would come to us.

"Laz, will my soul be trapped in the gate as well as yours if we don't succeed?"

He looked at me and smiled. "What did you just call me?"

"Laz? Is that not okay? It's what Gwen calls you, isn't it?"

"It is, and it's more than okay for you to use that as well."

"You. . .you'd prefer I call you Laz?"

He nodded. He hadn't stopped smiling. There was a look of delight in his eyes. Such a small thing seemed to have made him very happy.

"To answer your question, my fate, yes, yours, I don't think so. Any children we have, yes. It traps those of my blood. It may be Gwen's fate after death as well, even though she abdicated. Perhaps not, but the ring may still call her."

"So none of your family has an afterlife other than inside the ring and the manor."

"True. However, once we dismantle it, they'll have no other option but to cross over completely. In theory, at least."

"Will that change your magic?"

"I suspect that it will change things quite a bit. My inherent abilities aren't tied to that magic; neither are these new energies I'm using. Our bond isn't tied to the spirits either, so that will remain steady." He smiled. "In other words, you're stuck with me."

I threw my arms around his neck and settled myself on his lap. "I kinda like being stuck with you, *Laz*," I said, running my fingers through his hair.

"Do you now?"

"Yeah, you're okay. The sex is pretty awesome. I think I'll stay," I teased.

"So you only want me for my body?"

"Well, what you can do with it is pretty impressive too."

"Marjorie, whatever am I to do with you?"

"Mmm, I think whatever you like. I'm yours, after all."

"Yes, you are mine, and I say, we need to put these books aside and get to bed. Then I'll figure out what to do with you," he said as he leaned in for a quick kiss.

I slid off his lap and went about the business as instructed to put things away before getting into bed. He laughed as he slid in next to me. "You never cease to amaze me. You do as I ask so easily sometimes and then challenge me thoroughly other times."

I grinned, "And you love it, don't you?"

"Yes, I do."

I could tell he was exhausted after the day's events. I wondered if that oxygen-deprived episode had more of an effect on him than he was letting on. He was chatting more than usual, not pouncing on me. I knew if I initiated something, he'd go for it, but instead, I cuddled up to him, content to rest my head on his chest. And with that comfort, my beautiful husband drifted off to sleep quickly.

I lay awake for a while, turning over events and information in my head. What we'd found about dismantling the gate seemed too easy. I had to wonder why no one had ever done it before.

The Room

A sliver of light was beginning on the horizon outside the window. Lazlo was sound asleep next to me. It was a faint voice, but I couldn't understand the words. I slipped out of bed, threw on a robe, and looked out into the hallway.

A glowing figure was there. It turned to me, examining me; it spoke in a language I didn't understand, but I knew it wanted me to follow. I stepped into the hallway, and it started to drift further. I followed it and found myself in a section of the manor I hadn't seen before. It disappeared through a doorway. The door was locked when I tried it, but suddenly it opened. The glow from the spirit shone in the room, illuminating the room's contents.

The scene was horrifying. There were body parts preserved in jars on the shelf. Dust covered some surgical-looking instruments with sharp-looking edges that sat on a table. Next to it was a chair that featured decayed leather cuffs and ties. I noticed some footprints, more recent, in the dust on the floor. Narrow and slender, more feminine, and certainly not Lazlo's.

On the shelves, I noticed a few jars missing by the spaces and circles in the dust. Had Ana found this room or was Maeve in here? Or was there yet another individual hiding somewhere in this large manor?

The spirit spoke inside my head this time. "This is the family you married into. Their history is dark and deep. Your husband may be unaware on the surface, but there is darkness in his blood. Mark my words and tread carefully."

"He doesn't know about this room. I know he doesn't," I protested. Lazlo would never be part of something like this. It would horrify him as well.

"No, he does not, and perhaps showing him the dark potential will help him fight it. But be aware that it may also invite him to embrace it. Your lineage could tempt him in ways you cannot fathom. Your light, your power is already intoxicating to him even if he does not understand why."

I opened my mouth to protest, to ask what it was speaking of when the entity suddenly disappeared. The room went dark, although I could still see the hallway through the open door.

I made my way back to the bedroom with so many questions in my head. What lineage? My grandmother rarely mentioned my mother, so I had assumed that she was not magically inclined. Yet, the dragon had indicated she was a person of power. What was this other magical lineage?

When I walked back into the bedroom, Lazlo was still sleeping. He looked so peaceful and harmless. I couldn't believe for a moment he'd ever be capable of such atrocities, that anything in the world could change him into that.

I knew there was no way I could keep from showing him what I'd seen. If the spirit said it was a risk, I had to take it. I couldn't keep this secret from him. The spirit itself was a mystery. I hadn't seen an apparition other than the ancestors here, and this one was completely different. None of them had glowed. I hadn't been able to see much but had the feeling it had been a female in life.

As I sat there pondering, I watched the sun begin to cast its light across the grounds fully. A light tap at the door was Roland bringing in a morning tray. I put a finger to my lips to indicate quiet. Lazlo may have exaggerated when he said he got hours of sleep the previous night. His exhaustion and deep sleep seemed to show more of the truth. Roland nodded and quietly backed out.

I continued watching him sleep; looking at his breathing pattern, I began to breathe in sync with him. I watched him and concentrated. I felt a door opening.

"Not without permission," he had said about actually reading my mind. I backed off, fearing I was on the verge of crossing a similar line as it felt I was about to enter inside his head.

He stirred and began to open sleepy eyes, looking at me. "You got out of bed without me?" he said.

"I was awake, and you needed your sleep, so of course I did."

"Well, thank you. I suppose I was a bit lacking."

I brought the tray over to the bed and sat next to him.

"I hope you feel more rested now? I mean, we have been going full force for a few days now. Between our frolicking and your workouts, you are bound to need a break." I handed him a glass of juice off of the tray. He gave me a suspicious look.

"Last night you wanted me all to yourself. This morning, you let me sleep and now you're serving me. What is it that you want?"

I laughed. "Is that the way it was with your parents? Being sweet, kind, and loving doesn't have to mean I want something. It can mean I just appreciate you and care about you."

The trip to that room felt as if it had been a bad dream.

"Really? Last night you indicated your affections were more physical." He was enjoying this, teasing me about what I'd said.

"Well, perhaps I'm learning to love some of your other characteristics as well," I said. God, I adored this man.

He silently stared at me while finishing the drink in his hand and then handing me the empty glass. He leaned back in the bed, eyes still penetrating me. After a few moments of silence, he spoke.

"I'm glad to hear that. I know I certainly appreciate all of you." With that, I was tackled and pulled back onto the bed. We laughed as we wrestled a bit, me pretending to use moves that I had no desire to allow to work. We both used kisses and playful teasing as distractions, but I gave in pretty quickly, and he proved his energy was better restored with his vigorous and enthusiastic lovemaking.

We were still cuddling and touching each other when a knock came at the door. Lazlo made sure I was covered and then shouted. "Alright, come on in."

Roland peeked his head inside the doorway. "Miss Ana is asking for you, Sir." Lazlo and I exchanged a glance. I wondered what her answer would be this morning. I felt better after having at least one complete evening alone with Lazlo. It felt as if he and I had bonded further. I was glad that happened before the eerie room surfaced.

"Thank you, Roland. Please tell her we'll be out momentarily."

"Very good Sir, I will pass that along."

Lazlo turned to me. "See, she didn't sneak in here. No one did. Are you feeling better now?"

I nodded and smiled. "Much better."

He rose out of bed and began dressing. "Put your training

clothes back on. If Ana is leaving, I'll work with you. We need to keep up with your training."

I pulled out the clothes I'd worn the day before and began dressing. I had to show him the room. I couldn't avoid it. If I waited I'd only be distracted during training.

"Before we begin that, there's something I need to show you. Perhaps both of you. It was something a spirit guided me to see. It didn't look like any I've seen here at all. It was glowing, completely different. It called to me when I first woke up this morning."

He nodded, "Alright, we'll see what news Ana has, and then you can lead the way. We'd best not keep her waiting."

Ana was pacing the dining room when we arrived. "About time, guys! I know better than to ask what you were doing, however," she said.

"So, what's the decision?" Lazlo demanded of her. "Are you staying on and assisting me with Marjorie's training, or is your Goddess calling you away?"

"I'm assigned here for the moment," she said.

"Excellent." Lazlo turned to me. "Ana may be a tough instructor, but she's an excellent one. We've all benefitted from her style. Now that she has had much additional training, I can only imagine how much she has to offer as a teacher. But before we sit down or start working, I believe you have something to show us? Or was it just me you wanted?"

"Both of you, I think, need to see it."

We made our way back to where I'd been the night before. A wall now obstructed the hallway I had entered before. Intuitively I reached for Lazlo's hand and placed it on the wall. The illusion of the wall disappeared, and we were in the extended hallway. When I looked back at Lazlo, I wasn't sure if his look was of horror or simple disbelief that a hall he'd never seen existed.

"It was just open when I came here earlier," I explained.

When we came to the door, I again placed his hand on it, and it opened. A smell of death that I hadn't experienced earlier instantly overcame us. Ana turned pale and looked as if she was about to vomit. Lazlo had also lost color in his skin. At least I had my answer. Ana had not been here before, and Lazlo was clueless about the existence of this place. Lazlo waved his hand, the smell dissipated, and some lanterns inside lit, giving us a better view. They both looked quite disturbed at this chamber of horrors.

"Things are missing; they look like they were removed fairly recently," Lazlo noted.

"Yes, and I noticed footprints here." I pointed to the footprints in the dust.

"Mother. It had to be. How did she know this was here?"

"I don't know that she did. I suspect that the spirit inside her guided her here. This might have been his experimentation or torture room."

"I agree." Ana finally found her voice. "The sense I got about that spirit, this aligns with it. Evil, just evil."

"I still don't understand how you were led here," Lazlo said. "Why my ancestors wanted you to see this. It certainly paints my family in a poor light."

"The spirit warned me of darkness. Darkness, it said, is in your family's blood. It said that seeing this might help you fight it." I thought planting the more positive suggestion was the better way to go.

"Again, not at all sounding like any ancestor that has ever sent me a message. Plus, the magic you inherited connected you to your ancestors, not mine."

"It did speak of my lineage being involved, but I don't understand what it might have been referring to unless it has to do with my mother, who I know very little about."

"That would make a bit more sense but still odd that the spirit would be here. Unless, perhaps, it was killed here in this room or on these grounds."

A chill ripped through me. That wasn't a possibility I'd considered, that what I encountered was a ghost haunting this area.

"Based on what we are seeing, it appears more than one unfortunate individual met their demise here."

I noticed that Lazlo had either completely missed my suggestion he had a darkness inside him or chose to ignore it as he focused on other things. The smell was beginning to creep back in. Lazlo's spell was not containing it, and it was getting sickening.

"Ugh, guys, I can't take that smell in here," Ana confessed.

Lazlo nodded. "Yes, I'd prefer not to waste energy on it at the moment, so perhaps we should get out of here." He turned to me. "Let's see what we can find out about it if there are any records of who this was or what they were doing. It is darker than the darkest I ever witnessed Mother doing and rather sickening."

I was thankful to hear him voice the sickening part; what the spirit said was frightening. I couldn't imagine what could turn a person into this level of evil.

We left the area in silence, each of us lost in our individual thoughts. I wondered what was going through Lazlo's mind, what Ana was thinking, and what this all had to do with me. Why was this shown to me? The thought that what I saw was a ghost of someone who'd died in that room was frightening. Not the ghost part, but that they had died so horribly that something other than ancestral blood kept them bound to this location.

None of us seemed to feel like sitting down for any breakfast after that, perhaps I should have thought that part through first, but it was important to me not to carry that knowledge alone. I had to trust Lazlo and Ana too. At least now, I was sure it was not her sneaking into that room. That possibility had seemed unlikely, but I still knew precious little about her.

I could feel that experience hanging over everything we did. There was an absence of levity in all of us. Training with Ana, she seemed less frustrated with me, more patient, and compassionate. For my part, I gave her a much better effort. Lazlo dropped in, took over, gave me further pointers. I trained hard. Lazlo was also working on his powers while I worked with Ana. The blasts hitting the walls in varying strengths made it challenging for me to stay focused on the task at hand. Ana congratulated me on it. One thing bothering me was that Lazlo was avoiding eye contact with me. Even when we sparred together and it was necessary, I sensed he had a wall up, keeping me out.

Keeping it Together

Ana joined us for dinner. The conversation was light, mostly about training, and most of the talking was done by Ana. As we were parting, Lazlo was about to make his excuses to do his evening training routine. I knew it was coming. I spoke first.

"Laz, before you go, I need to talk to you. Alone."

If we were going to keep this relationship together, I'd best do my part and not allow this feeling to continue.

"Certainly," he replied. He was tense. I could see it in his body and hear it in that simple word.

"In the study?" He nodded and followed me. Ana went her own way.

We walked into that room, and, as he had before when he wanted my undivided attention, I closed the door. There was a sadness in his eyes, perhaps even a tinge of fear as if he thought I would say something he didn't want to hear.

I held his hands in mine, looking up at his face. His eyes met mine. "I can tell something is wrong. I don't want to lose you. Please talk to me."

I wanted so much just to tell him I loved him. The words were stuck, but this was as close as I was getting for now.

His eyes shifted. The tension, the look of dread all disappeared. He held my hand and led me to the small divan in front of the fireplace. We sat down together.

"I thought that you doubted me, that you worried that I'd become a monster. That you wouldn't want to be with me, knowing that risk."

"I'd be lying if I said that what the spirit told me didn't cause me concern. It does. But you are my husband now. I'm not going anywhere. If anything does surface, we can fight it together."

His grip tightened on my hands. "I'm sorry I doubted you. I've never had anyone want to truly be there for me, well, not in that manner," he said.

Suddenly I had an awareness of him. He was the eldest child. As a son, instead of the daughter his mother wanted, he was set aside. His mother molded him as she saw fit. When his sister wanted out, he thought nothing of sacrificing himself for her needs. Our marriage, one thing he'd wanted himself, had been his mother's will in the end. She'd even taken that choice away from him.

He'd borne all of it with acceptance as a way of life but still had managed to become his own man. He hadn't mentioned his father much, but I imagined he'd been an important figure to Lazlo, although it didn't seem as if they had been close. The only person close to him had been his sister, and she'd left him. When all of this came flooding into my mind, I suddenly felt awful that I had treated him the way I had, going back and forth with my affections. Lazlo had shown me nothing but kindness, heroism, and love.

"I'm sorry if my wishy-washy nature caused you doubt or concern. I was so caught up in my internal drama. I never stopped to think about how things were for you, how unsettling hearing what that spirit said to me had to be for you as well. I'm sorry I allowed you to doubt me."

I felt I'd told him enough about the spirit's warning. The whole, my energy being intoxicating part, sounded like nothing I wanted to share. His demeanor was back to normal.

"Yes, I suppose we both have much to learn, don't we? Like you, I've not entered into this depth with anyone."

"But over the last decade, you've surely had a girlfriend or two?"

"Mother attempted to arrange others. My military duties and absence usually sent them away in a fairly short amount of time. They favored others who would shower them with affection, where I never felt so motivated. Not until I reunited with you, that is. There's something here, Marjorie, something bigger than either of us."

Was he right in believing we were somehow destined for each other or was it my energy he coveted? I couldn't deny I was attracted to Lazlo from the moment I arrived here. Sure, I did my best to deny it, but it didn't take long before giving in to my feelings. I felt displaced here, a stranger. I remembered more of my childhood the longer I was here, but that last time I was here when things were different between us, nothing.

Lazlo made it sound like Gran grabbed me and ran. Perhaps she found out about that room? That would terrify anyone. But then why send Lazlo a message to find me after her death?

"I agree. On some level, it feels as if we're pawns in someone else's master plan. There's a reason your Mother wanted us together beyond what she stated, or perhaps it was the spirit. Either way, I think we will need to guard each other well. Something is amiss. That much I can sense."

I knew choosing my words wisely was important. Not for

one second did I want Lazlo to think I was backing down. Being committed to that was an essential part of any chance we had of overcoming whatever we would face together. My natural inclination was to waiver, but I had to set that aside. We were in this together. I was sticking by his side.

"Agreed, I sense it as well. It's unsettling to think that. However, I am curious about one thing."

"What is that?"

"If my mother hadn't intervened, would you have said yes to my proposal?"

I laughed. "We'd still be hooking up, and I'd still be tormenting you." I teased. "I wouldn't have given in this quickly on my own. Eventually though, yeah, you'd probably win."

He smiled broadly. "That's good to hear."

"On a different topic, were you planning on training more with Ana tonight?"

"Only if you don't need me."

I nodded. "I'm fine. Don't keep her waiting any longer. I want to do some research on my own in the main library, and then I'll go to bed. You'll be late, I assume?"

He nodded. "Very likely. I train on my own mostly, so having someone to watch or work with is a bonus I don't get that often."

We exchanged a heartfelt kiss and a long embrace before we parted ways.

The Gift

After his departure, I made my way to the main library. Closing my eyes, I asked the library to lead me to information on my mother. I felt a presence and opened my eyes. It seemed to be the same spirit who'd appeared to me before, or at least it was pretty similar in fashion. Several books in the room were glowing.

"Beware of the knowledge you seek. Knowing is not always the best path," she warned. "not unless you can guard it safely."

"You mean not tell anyone."

"At this point, yes. The men in this family of blood lineage have not done well, particularly the firstborn sons. As you've already discovered, some of the women can often struggle as well. These books contain some of their histories, although this family does not speak ill of itself much. It covers up more than it admits."

"So you are not one of them?"

"No, I perished inside that room. The spirit that has escaped tortured, mutilated, and finally killed me. My energy lives, a result of his experiments. Wards in this manor are why I cannot leave."

"Is there anything I can do to help?"

"Seal or dismantle the gate, then the wards inside will

crumble, and I will be free."

"That's our plan; extract the wayward spirit, send it through, and dismantle the gate so that the spirits cross over."

Some of the spirit's features were more apparent. It was less glowing, definitely a woman. The entity was primarily white with a soft yellow glow about her. As it hovered in the air, I wasn't sure if it had wings or if that was another trick of the light. I had the sense that it hadn't been human in life. It reminded me of the white lady in the woods, although still different.

"It is a good plan. It will serve you well."

There was a burning question on my mind. "Are you my ancestor?"

"Very long ago, further back than most remember, but your people are related to my people. In that regard, I have called someone here to help you."

From behind her glow appeared a child, a young boy with leaves circling his head and wings on his back. His eyes were large and bright, and he smiled broadly. He spoke in a language I didn't understand.

"He says he is honored to meet you and is bringing you a gift," The spirit said.

In his hands, the boy held a white box. He opened it and pulled out a ball of golden light. The box floated in the air as he left it there and walked toward me, hands extended and full of the light. He stopped in front of me and raised the light to just below my navel. The light left his hand and suddenly entered my body. I could feel it inside me, lighting me up internally. It felt as if it was more fully restoring my connection to my magic. I stood there stunned until the intensity died down.

I looked at the boy, trusting that either he would understand or, once again, the spirit would translate. "I'm honored to meet you also and thank you for bringing your gift. What can I do for you in return?" I asked.

He replied again in his language. Clearly, he understood me, and I was the one who was lacking.

"He says to be joyful, be happy, and love well. Those are his wishes for you. The gift was sent from your grandfather and comes with no attachment as all gifts should," the spirit said.

The young boy then disappeared as quickly as he had appeared. I could still feel my insides glowing. It felt as if I was being filled with energy. I looked around, and I was alone again. The spirit had also disappeared, but the books were still glowing. The gift he had implanted in me seemed to be absorbed now.

I called to the spirit again. What did she mean by my grandfather? Was it a gift beyond the grave or a living person I'd never met? There was no response this time.

Instead, I turned to the books, pulling them off of the shelves and onto a table. For the next several hours, I flipped through pages, unsure what I was seeking. Reading one section, I momentarily lost my breath. The manor was built on a magical hot site. There were caverns beneath it that also contained massive intersections of ley lines, the lines through which the energy of the magic flow. The unique placement of this manor had allowed for the gate. It wouldn't have worked with less magical access.

One of the books I pulled out I was almost afraid to open. It was dusty, the cover was ragged, and it'd been hidden back behind several others. If I hadn't been following that glow, I would've missed it. When I opened it, the cover felt brittle, almost as if it would turn to dust if I weren't careful. This was Maximillian's journal. What I read inside was frightening. While the family was doing different experiments with the grounds, the ley lines, and plant life, Maximillian worked with creatures that held magic. The room we saw was his laboratory, where he worked in secret. That was why he was imprisoned. The book notes had an addendum that had to have been added after his death. The notes were still very old but contained different energy. Someone had found these notes and continued his work. There was a good chance that the spirit inside Maeve was either Maximillian himself or this unnamed second ancestor who had continued his work.

I decided reading more was not what I wanted to see. I took that old book and created a nook in which to hide it. After what I'd just learned, Lazlo was not someone I wanted to read these contents. As much faith as I had in him until I could understand these magics better it wasn't worth the risk.

I put away the others where they belonged and headed back to our room.

Healing Magic

I awoke when Lazlo entered the bedroom and slammed the door. He didn't undress but came straight from the door to the bed and fell into it as if he was exhausted. I reached over for him, and he acknowledged me. His chest was wet. His breathing was irregular.

As my hand ran across him, I felt him wince. The wet didn't feel like sweat; it was sticky. The metallic smell was sickeningly familiar. I summoned light. I nearly vomited at the sight before me. There was blood everywhere. His shirt was drenched, he had several large lacerations oozing across his chest. He was barely conscious, uttering a few moans. It was late. It was likely that everyone else was asleep. I wasn't sure how to summon help. I had to try something on my own.

I closed my eyes and concentrated. Power began building inside me, more power than I'd been able to summon since I'd been here, more coursing through me than ever before. The shimmering gold light was all around me. I was hoping it could heal him as I poured it into him. The wound began to close. When the magic sealed it, I grabbed towels to clean him to make sure the bleeding had stopped. He was still delirious from blood loss. He opened his eyes a little. He tried to say my name, or at least I think he did, but it came out as a grunt. I put my hands on him again, pouring more into him to accelerate his healing. After a few minutes, his breathing was returning to normal. His eyes opened; this time, there was more clarity.

"Marjorie," he whispered.

"I'm here," I replied. "Stay still; you need rest."

The bed was a mess, and the floor wasn't looking too good, either. He'd dripped blood on the floor as he'd made his way to the bed. I didn't dare leave his side just yet.

I wanted to yell at him for being careless. I wanted to throttle Ana for hurting him without healing him. Still, it was totally out of character for her to have cut him like that and let him walk away. The wound also didn't match any weapon I'd seen her use, but what else could explain this?

Lazlo was in no condition for me to ask him. He was better, he wasn't going to die, but the magic needed more time to fully heal him.

Lazlo looked at me through his half-closed eyes. "Not Ana, Marjorie," he said as if reading my mind. "It wasn't her."

"Tell me later. Don't force it now. Rest."

Then I heard it, an unearthly sound, not quite a growl but terrifying.

"Bolt the door, quickly." Lazlo tried to get off the bed. I stopped him and went for the door. Before I managed to bolt it, I saw yellow eyes in the hallway through the crack, some sort of animal. I heard it throwing itself at the closed door.

"Where the hell did that come from?" I practically shouted at him.

Lazlo pulled himself up in the bed. He was summoning his strength, pulling in his power.

"Can you hit me with your healing again, or is it draining you? We'll need all our combined strength if that thing makes it in here."

He was becoming more lucid by the minute. I was thankful for that, especially with this strange new threat outside the door. He glanced at me, his eyes steady on the door.

"You're naked. Grab something, anything, the thicker, the better. Cover yourself. Do that first,"

In all of this insanity, I'd forgotten that. I pulled out a coat and threw it on, and grabbed another one for Lazlo. To my surprise, he reached underneath the bed and pulled out an axe. I'd wondered what he'd do for a weapon other than magic and had no idea that that was stored in the bedroom.

"Never mind the healing. No time." The thumps on the door were getting louder. It was getting more determined. I wasn't sure how long that door would hold, with both of us somewhat depleted magically. We heard a scream, a yowl, and then silence—next, a knock at the door.

"You guys okay in there? What the hell was that thing?"

Lazlo visibly relaxed. "Ana," he said and turned to me.

"I'll get the door; you sit," I instructed him.

When I opened the door, there she was, standing over the carcass of a grotesque creature. It had spikes all down its back and long talons extended from both its front and back legs. Ana's sword was lodged in its deformed skull. As she pulled it out, I saw a different glowing white figure behind her. It looked at me, and I could tell it was thanking us as if its spirit had been trapped inside this beast. At least, that was the message I sensed coming through. It lingered for a moment, then it disappeared. Ana showed no indication she was aware of anything other than what was there physically in the hallway.

"I couldn't sleep, so I went for a walk. I don't usually come over here but had this weird feeling and then saw this beast trying to break down your door."

She held my eyes, knowing that as thankful that I was that she had come to our aid, I had to be wondering why she was anywhere near our bedroom. Was she protective or did her Goddess figure into her decision?

"Whose blood is this?" she asked.

The light I had set in the bedroom spilled into the dark hallway, illuminating the trail of blood Lazlo had left on his way here.

"It didn't come from this creature," Ana said.

"That would be mine," Lazlo said from inside the room.

She looked at me, then inside the door at Lazlo, then back at me. The look in her eyes said she realized the extent of blood loss and was surprised to see him looking so well. She knew it had to be because of me that he was alive. She stepped over the creature's body and into the doorway, leveling her eyes at Lazlo.

"Care to explain anything, big guy? Like what the hell?"

The look on Lazlo's face was one of guilt. "After I left you, I went back to that room to look around. Yes, I know I shouldn't have, but I felt I needed to know more about what Mother had been doing in there." His speech was slow but deliberate. I know I was glaring at him. I felt Ana was too.

"So I heard a noise, touched something, and then this thing sprung out at me."

"And, of course, you were unarmed, dimwit." Ana shook her head.

He shrugged. "In my defense, I thought all that was in there was dust and gruesome bottles," he said.

"So why go back there at all?" I asked.

"I wanted to see if I could figure out what Mother had taken. I thought perhaps it might be of importance to us."

"You might've told me. I'd have gone with you," Ana said.

Lazlo shrugged. "I didn't think of it until I was passing there. When the creature escaped, I got out of the room."

"Well, that's at least one smart thing you did," Ana said.

Lazlo ignored her comment. "I tried to get it to follow me toward the practice area in hopes of grabbing a weapon, but it ran in the opposite direction, headed to where Marjorie was. So I ran after it, engaged it against my better judgment, it tore a chunk out of me, but I got away and managed to take a shortcut back to the room and beat it here."

I wanted to slap him. In my mind, I did. Asshole. In reality, I stood there, silent and dumbfounded.

Ana, though, was not lost for words. "You wrestled with that thing? Fuck. You are one lucky son of a bitch, Lazlo. Lucky that you got here, and by the blood pattern on the floor, bed, and your shirt, I'd say lucky your woman here has mad healing skills. Call me impressed, Marjorie. You patched up his idiocy nicely."

My glare softened as I looked at him, his breathing was still somewhat labored. He wasn't standing.

"I wasn't sure he would make it," I said. I realized at that moment, now that the immediate crisis was over, that I'd nearly lost him.

Hours before, I had so wanted to confess to him that I loved him and I'd failed. And then, so soon afterward, he almost died without me ever letting him know.

I crossed to Lazlo, and he grasped my hand. "I'm sorry," he said.

I nodded, then held his eyes with mine. "Don't you ever do

that again. I'm furious at you, but you need to rest, so you're getting a break." I gently pushed him back onto the bed. He would live, but his body needed to recover, not just from the trauma but from the massive influx of magic I'd poured into him.

"I'll take care of this thing in the hallway. I'll also search to make sure Lazlo didn't inadvertently release anything else in his bravado back there," Ana said, shooting Lazlo a look that could only be described as condescending. He didn't make any effort to respond.

I wanted to get to the kitchen for some supplies. Lazlo might need more attention. With Ana's mention of possible other things, I thought an armed escort might be advisable.

"Do you mind walking with me to the kitchen? I want to get a few things to brew a tea to help with the healing and make sure he sleeps."

"Sure," Ana said. "I'll head that way with you and back. Just to be safe."

I turned to Lazlo and kissed him gently. "Please sleep. I'll be back with something to help in case you need it."

We walked down the hall in an awkward silence. At least I felt awkward.

"Ana," I said at last, breaking the tension, "thank you for being here, for helping me, and for protecting us."

She smiled. "It's okay. I know you aren't that comfortable with me. You don't know or understand much of our ways and certainly not of my order. I'm here because it is the will of the Goddess, not because I am trying to interfere in any matters going on here."

For some reason, I just unloaded. "I know. I know a lot on a logical level. I know I'm an outsider, a stranger. I also know I've never been involved with anyone on the level I am with Lazlo. Hell, I never even had a long-term relationship, and now I'm here, apparently forever, married to him. I mean, geez, what sort of woman waits until after she is married to realize she loves her husband? Me, apparently. How in hell am I supposed to keep him happy?"

"Look, before I met you, I'd heard your name. I'd heard Gwen speak of his love for you, and when I saw him with you at the tavern, it was all over his face. All you need to do is love him back, that's what he wants, even I can see that," Ana said.

I wanted her words to make me feel better. They should have, but all I could think about was the warning I'd received from the spirit that my energy was addictive to him. And what about my response to Lazlo? Something about him drew me as well. I realized that part did make me feel better. This wasn't one-sided. The spirit was wrong. This had two sides; we were both drawn to each other, even if I had attempted to hide or deny it at first.

I was relieved that we neither saw nor heard anything strange on our way to and from the kitchen. I gathered my supplies without incident, and when we returned, Lazlo had drifted into a deep sleep. I wished I had changed the blood-soaked bedsheets, but certainly did not want to disturb him. Magic seemed the best solution to tidy them up. I was thankful to be running full force, even stronger than before. I wondered if it had to do with that golden light gift, or perhaps my new knowledge of the lay lines beneath the manor was another addition. I could feel myself drawing from them.

"So, are you alright here, then?" Ana asked as I did my best to fix things without disturbing Lazlo.

"Yes, Ana, I am. Thank you." Suddenly I felt self-centered.

Ana had saved our lives, and here I did nothing for her.

"Ana, are you okay? Is there anything that I can do for you? You've done so much for me. For us."

"You're sweet. Truly you are. I am fine, basically," she said. "Perhaps slightly insane, if you listen to Lazlo, but you know, getting by."

"Do you mind if I ask a few things?" Now I was curious.

"Go on," Ana said, sitting in a chair. She seemed open to discussion.

"You use magical artifacts, but I've never seen you use magic. You must have some ability, or you couldn't even use those. Is that correct?"

She smiled. "Correct. I come from a magical family, but my magical aptitude wasn't up to expectations so, after I turned eighteen, my family sent me here to train with Lazlo's father. That's how I met this family. My family wanted to have me trained as a warrior."

"It certainly explains why the two of you have such similar fighting styles as well."

She nodded. "Yes, Jordan would have me train with Lazlo as well. He was my primary teacher, but I learned a lot from that sleeping lug over there."

This was the first time I'd even heard anyone say Jordan's name since I'd been here. I remembered him vaguely. He was a tall man, muscular like his son. He had been handsome from what I recalled and relatively quiet next to his more charismatic wife.

"We went to war together. His father and I were in the same unit. Lazlo was in a different unit, but we all three met up on the battlefield. I owe them both a lot."

I sensed a void in Ana. Something unsaid, a secret she was

keeping.

"You've been to war?"

"Yes, and it feels as if another may not be far off. My order is aligned with King Mordecai. If he gets attacked, I'll get called to action."

I felt a twinge of familiarity at the mention of that name. It was more than simply having heard it before. I knew something. I saw a flash of a face, a smile.

"Have you met him? King Mordecai?"

She nodded. "He swears us into the order. He's a fair man and cares about his people. He's also immensely powerful. I think that's the only reason he hasn't been attacked yet," she said.

Ana got out of the chair and headed for the door. "If you are alright, I'd like to complete a round and get some rest myself."

"Of course," I said, "if there is anything I can do for you, please ask. I don't know you well enough to know what you might need, but my talents are here for you."

"And from what I've seen, your talents are extensive. For now, watch over the big guy. Gwen would kill me if I let her brother die on my watch. Re-bolt the door after I leave. I think we're safe, but I'll check again. Get some sleep." And with that, she left the room.

I turned to Lazlo. His eyes were open. I wondered how much of our conversation he had heard. "Hi," he said as I slid into bed next to him.

"How are you feeling?"

"Tired, sleepy, but glad you are here."

"I wouldn't be anywhere else. I brought some herbs and tea things if you have trouble sleeping."

He wrapped his arms around me, his eyelids heavy with

oncoming sleep as I stroked his hair.

"Sleep now," I suggested, and he drifted back off to sleep.

Something is Coming

The sun was already up when I awoke. There was no morning tray. I knew Roland had gone out for the night, but usually, he was here in the morning. I got out of bed. Lazlo stirred. While I was dressing, his eyes were watching me. I turned to him.

"How are you feeling this morning? You seem to have slept well."

"Yes, thanks to you and your skills, I'm alive and feeling normal," he said.

"Normal is a stretch. Let the magic do its work. Those were some nasty injuries you had, and you lost a good amount of blood as well."

He looked around the room. "Has Roland not been in?"

"No, he hasn't. I thought perhaps he had a day off or something?"

"He didn't ask for one. He knows I'd have granted it if he had. It's very unlike him not to be here. I hope everything is alright."

Lazlo rose and peeled off the torn shirt he had slept in. I could see the faint outlines of his lacerations. They would heal and disappear, but for now, they were a reminder of the terror of last night.

SOMETHING IS COMING

There was a knock at the door.

"Guys, we have a problem," Ana's voice said from the hallway. I opened the door, and she entered the room. "Look outside."

We all three went to the window. The sight was horrifying. Lazlo had built a border to keep the hunter children out, but there they were, all over that border, clinging to it. I could feel their eyes piercing the walls of the manor. It was sickening. There were so many of them, layers of them, and they appeared to be scaling the invisible wall.

"Well, that explains why Roland isn't here. I can't blame him. We're on our own here today. My staff knows I don't expect any of them to go near such a thing, and none of them stayed here last night."

The children were getting to the top of the invisible wall and falling over the edge. They disintegrated as they fell toward the ground.

"We'd best get ready," Ana said. "Something's coming. Your mother or something else. But something. These things can't be here on their own."

Ana's voice was tense. Her hand was on the sword at her side. I could feel her heartbeat rising. I'd never sensed that in anyone before, but now it seemed I was more finely tuned to emotions around me. She was worried about what this meant, about what was coming.

"Agreed," Lazlo said. "Preparation is key. We should all be dressed for battle, just in case. Marjorie that means you should get into your training clothes. I don't think we need to go full armor, but we need to be able to move freely."

Ana left to continue her patrol while Lazlo and I dressed. The scene beyond the window continued to get worse. More and more of them. One dropped and didn't disintegrate. It started walking toward the manor, more were following.

"I'm too depleted to keep that border strong enough for that onslaught," Lazlo confessed. "We should be able to keep them outside the walls, but we're trapped inside until we can summon enough magic to banish them."

I wondered if I already had that capacity. Still, we didn't know yet what was drawing them here. I had my suspicions that it had to do with the gift I had received. From what Lazlo said, these beings were drawn to fairy magic, and the little boy with leaves in his hair and wings on his back certainly fit that description. If so, the gift he gave me was fairy magic, and right now, Lazlo and I were both radiating fairy energy. That couldn't be good under the circumstances, and me using more of it could potentially make things worse. I had to wonder about the motives of the entity that had brought me this gift. Had she known what would happen? Suddenly I felt a pull to go back to that room. Something or someone was calling me. It felt helpful as if there was something there I'd need and soon.

I put my hand on his arm. "I know this may sound crazy, but I need to go back to that room." As suspected, he looked at me as if I was insane. "I know it seems counterintuitive, but I need to go, and I need you to get me there. Just don't touch anything once we get there."

"Marjorie," he began to object. I could tell by his stern look.

"Please don't argue with me. Just trust me." I pleaded.

"We're not going near that room until I'm armed."

I nodded. "Okay, grab your weapons and meet me in that hallway. I'll wait outside for you." There was nothing there to hurt us. I sensed it, I knew it.

"No, wife. You are coming with me. No choice," he said.

I sighed. "Wife is my name now?"

"A reminder Marjorie. I'm your husband and your protector. You need to respect that."

His tone was unmistakable. I wasn't winning this one. I was going to the weapons room with him.

When we entered the practice room, Lazlo went about selecting weapons for both of us. I took the dagger he handed me. Something inside my head was still screaming at me to go back to that room.

Once he was happy, I made my point again. "Can we go there now? Something could be there that we need."

He nodded. He secured his weapons and mine, took my hand, and we headed back toward that frightening room.

Souvenirs

Entering the room, it was clear something had happened here when the beast was unleashed. Instead of dust and the smell of death, we saw swirling lights. The air was thick with them. Several of the jars were shattered on the floor, light beaming out of the remnants. A scent of forest lingered. This could be another thing drawing those hunters here.

"Stay here. Don't move," I instructed. Lazlo nodded. Stepping over fluid and broken glass, I went to a cabinet on the wall. The lights in the air were following me, dancing around my fingers as I reached for the latch. What was inside was spectacular but also haunting. I'd watched enough television and seen enough documentaries to know it is common for serial killers to keep mementos of their victims. This cabinet seemed to be where this one kept his. The cabinet contained perfectly aligned and displayed jewelry. There were pendants, rings, and bracelets, all of incredible craftsmanship.

"Marjorie," Lazlo said from outside the room, "Mother is coming. I can hear her. I should get down there and deal with her myself."

The lights were soothing. I knew I was safe there. "I think I've found what I was after." The lights danced around a light green glowing pendant and a pink ring. They seemed to be calling to me. As I picked them up, they were warm to the touch. After pocketing them, I headed back to Lazlo.

"Can you get to the gate room alone? I prefer not to leave your side, but it may be easier for me to get Mother to the gate room if I am leading her there by myself. Then we can free her and seal the gate."

My heart was racing. Were we already at that point? Was she here?

I nodded. "Yes, I can find my way. Ana is here somewhere, so I know I can call her if I have a problem. I'll see if I can get her down there as well."

"Good plan," he said. He pulled me in and kissed me quickly. "I will see you down there, wife." He smiled. Apparently, that was now his code for "do as I say."

I made my way through the narrow hallways, navigating myself intuitively. It was as if I could tap into the energetics here and get whatever I needed. I'd never felt so powerful before. I'd hoped that my new spirit friend might surface to aid us, but she was nowhere to be seen.

Entering the gate room, again, I marveled at how it reminded me of an aquarium, or perhaps an undersea viewing room. The huge stone ring and the energy pulsating in and around it reminded me of water with its aqua color and shimmering hue. Behind it, beings were floating that resembled fish in a sea of energy. There were larger ones and smaller ones, and they even varied in color. Previously when I entered here, they paid me little attention, but this time it felt like they were all congregating at the front. Were they staring at me? Can spirits do that? I moved closer to the entrance. They backed off as if they were somehow afraid of me.

"Marjorie," I heard Lazlo's voice behind me. I turned to see him, his mother beside him. Suddenly a flash of light enveloped me, and everything went black.

Truths

My head ached. Pain shot down my neck. The surface beneath me and behind me felt cold. I tried to move my head but then sensed a restraint across it. As my eyes began to open, the room was still swirling. Oh, god, my head hurt. My hands wouldn't move, nor would my feet. I felt sick as the fear began to build inside me.

"There she is," Maeve cooed right in front of my face. "Nice of you to join us, dear."

Lazlo was standing further back. He appeared to be staring at nothing. This room seemed similar to the other room we had found, far less antiquated from what I could see of it. Since I couldn't move my head, my vision was limited, but none of this looked good.

"Aw, you look confused, daughter-in-law. I'll do you a favor and enlighten you. My darling son here is Lord of the estate. That status and magic make him a prime candidate for a ride-along ancestor who is in there having a good chat with him as we speak. Poor Lazlo hasn't experienced this yet. Eventually, he'll figure out how to free himself. It isn't easy the first time, very difficult, in fact without proper training. His new friend is explaining all the things we need Lazlo to hear. Things we figured out. Like you have no plans to give him any children, do you? Can you even? Not that you would know, but after encountering the men you did, I doubt it. Oh, yes, I know all about that. My son can keep nothing from me. Then there is the matter of your lineage. You probably don't even know the whole truth of that, but I suspect you are beginning to figure it out."

I began to speak, to protest. "What -"

"Oh, save your strength, dear. You are going to need it," she said as she pressed me back into the cold metal chair.

"I'll enlighten you. Your mother was one of the Fae stragglers, the ones that didn't disappear right away. I suspect the rest of her family was hiding elsewhere when she encountered your father, fell in love, blah blah blah."

She looked at me, then looked at a variety of stones she had set out on the table. She selected one and turned back to me. "It's admittedly unusual for a Fae and a human to produce children, so you were something of a miracle baby. Too bad about you, though. It would have been beneficial to our family to mix blood like that. Not only the magics but that book you have too." She sighed and selected another crystal. "But back to you as the baby. You see, your mother's family was none too happy at the blood mix. They attempted to trap her to bring her back to them. She was caught in that trap when your father sought aid and stumbled upon the cult known as The Collectors. They assured him they could free his beloved and return her to him."

"Collectors? I've not heard nice things about them." After what I'd seen in that room, their name now sounded even more horrifying.

Maeve shrugged. "The price, however, was their child, you, Marjorie." She lifted a strand of my hair. "The miracle baby."

TRUTHS

I looked at her in horror. The idea that they'd wanted me as a baby was sickening.

She selected another crystal. "Your father agreed, despite your mother's objections from inside her cage. It was your grandmother who crossed them to save you, and in that deed, your father and mother both perished at the hands of The Collectors."

I sat there blinking, unable to move even if I wanted to but stunned at the same time by all she was telling me. My grandmother sacrificed her only child to save me? Suddenly I felt terrible for suggesting to her that I didn't want to continue our family line. Being able to do that seemed more important than it ever was to me before.

"Oh, don't worry, Lazlo can hear all of this too. He needs to know who you are, who he wanted. When your grandmother first came here with you, I had no idea who she was, who you were. I'd heard the story even though I wasn't part of that cult. I had no idea, nor did they, of the lineage of the man that had come to them, desperate for their help."

I looked at Lazlo. He was still just standing there, staring into space. He didn't seem particularly aware of much.

"Of course, when your grandmother came here, I knew who she was. She helped me a great deal with many wonderful recipes in her book. When Lazlo asked for the marriage, I assumed you were merely a human girl he'd fallen for who was magically gifted and could use that wonderful book."

My book, summoning it now wouldn't help me. My hands were bound. Maeve would just hand it to Lazlo, who could read it now that we were married. Could I remember a spell to give me extra strength? I had a sense I would need something.

"When your grandmother crossed paths with one of The

Collectors on a visit here, I learned the whole truth of both of you. It was at that point that she spirited you away, and we never saw you again. Poor Lazlo was rather heartbroken. At any rate, none of this truly matters, but as my daughter-in-law, I did want you to have some understanding of why we need to do what we need to do."

I was nervous to ask. "What do you need to do?"

"Well, we've managed to drain all the fairy magic you loaded into Lazlo out of him. Now we need to drain you. Of course, Lazlo has plenty of other magic in his veins, so taking that out didn't hurt him at all, but you, well, you may or may not survive the process. Well, survive as in having much of a life. We need you *somewhat* living so that book doesn't disappear before we can remove that spell from it."

Maeve had a solid understanding of the way the book's magic worked. She wasn't under the illusion that it would be bound to Lazlo if I died.

She brought the crystals over and began to attach them to my hands, feet, and the strap against my head and neck as well. When I looked over at Lazlo, I could see the strain on his face. Veins were bulging in his neck. He appeared to be fighting inside somewhere.

Maeve sighed. "Well, dear, I would say this won't hurt, but I'd be lying, and you deserve the truth. It won't be terrible at first, but it will get worse. Pity, but Lazlo will get over it and get on with it. He can decide if he still wants you or wants to set you aside. It won't matter to me. He'll need to get together with someone who can pop out a baby for him. Whether or not he is married to her won't matter. So you see, there are plenty of solutions."

I watched as she cast a spell on the gemstones attached to

me. I could feel the heat at each spot as it began to pull the magic out of me. She examined her work and seemed pleased.

She leaned in and whispered to me. "Of course, if he can't manage to banish his ride-along ancestor for a while, then your future is quite glum, I fear. He'll have no use for you other than body parts once we've solved the book issue if Lazlo doesn't fight him off in time."

I kept attempting to subtly wriggle a hand free of the restraint. It was tight, but they were leather, so I knew there would be some give. It was worth a try. The amulet was still around my neck, Maeve was apparently still unable to see it. If I could reach it there was a chance I could use its power to release Lazlo. The question remained whether or not I could accomplish that on my own, even if I could break free.

Was the spirit inside him the same one that had been inside Maeve? She seemed in complete control. I could feel the ring and pendant I had picked up from the other room lighting up with energy. Maeve's magic seemed to be going for the artifacts first, which gave me a small window before it started invading me. I couldn't access my magic; whatever she did seemed to be interfering.

I knew above all I couldn't give in to panic, but still, the tears began to roll. Partly fear, partly frustration, mostly fear. It was as if Lazlo never saved me from those men, and they had succeeded in selling me, and this was my fate. I wasn't sure which was worse, the threat of being raped over and over or being drained of magic and dismembered.

NO! I am a survivor. I was a miracle baby. My grandmother sacrificed everything to save me. I was loved, cherished. Lazlo was fighting. I could see the strain and how difficult it was for the spirit to maintain control. If only I could get close to him.

I continued to wiggle my wrist back and forth, thankful for my small slender hands. I might get one hand free, but would it be in time, and what would I be able to accomplish? Since I had nothing to lose, I kept at it, making sure my efforts couldn't be noticed.

"Hello, Maeve." I heard Ana's voice from somewhere in the shadows as she stepped forward, sword in hand.

"Well, well, well, if it isn't the little slut herself," Maeve replied. "How dare you show your face here. Or have you moved on to my son now that he's married?"

"What did you do to him?" Ana shot a glance at both me and Lazlo.

"Oh, Lazlo? Nothing really beyond allowing him to host a powerful spirit. Or did you mean Jordan? He is living his best life as a wolf currently. I thought it suited him, especially since I left him turning human for three nights a month during the full moon. Delicious, don't you think? Part-time wolf hunted by men, part-time man hunted by wolves." Maeve taunted, clearly trying to upset Ana. "He's still alive though. I'd feel it if he wasn't." I could see the two women beginning to circle each other.

"Lazlo darling, please tend to our guest in the chair," she said, as her circle moved her further away from me and closer to Ana. So far, the gemstones were pulling energy out of the artifacts in my pocket. It was surprising they had that much in them, or perhaps they'd been recharged when that beast was freed. Was that why they'd called me? They knew what I'd face? I sensed that their energy was getting low, and I'd be feeling this soon enough.

Despite the resistance I had seen in Lazlo earlier, there was zero resistance to him approaching me as instructed. I hoped that was because that was one thing he did not want to resist, being closer to me. I noted that Maeve had not referred to me by my name or my relationship to Lazlo, keeping as distant as possible when sending him over. Still, she seemed confident enough in the spirit's control over him to send him to me where I might actually have a chance to help him break free. Or perhaps she assumed I was already helpless. My right hand was nearly free. I stopped moving it out of fear that the spirit in Lazlo might notice, but although he dutifully checked the levels, he paid me no more attention as he appeared distracted by Ana and Maeve's confrontation.

"Is that your motive, Maeve? To suck any chance of joy or happiness out of everyone around you?" Ana said.

"What happiness, little whore? Did you think he was going to run away with you? No, he confessed his indiscretion and begged for my forgiveness. No thought to you or the brat – his brat - that he said you were carrying."

"You are lying!"

"Am I? Well, only a lone wolf somewhere in a forest might be able to say otherwise." With that, she threw a bolt of magic energy at Ana, who quickly sidestepped it, allowing it to disintegrate a section of the wall. Maeve wasn't playing; she meant to kill Ana.

Suddenly I felt it. The artifacts were dead. I bit my lip so as not to cry out and draw any attention to myself. Better Maeve and the spirit thought I was already suffering; my tear-streaked face had given them that impression.

"Laz, please," I managed, hoping to bring him back to me. My hand came free, but I left it in place so as not to draw attention in case the spirit in control noticed and simply re-secured me, but the pain was getting worse, and even though I'd freed my hand, the gem nearest to it was still pulling into me.

He turned his eyes to mine. I could see the conflict, the battle. Fighting the pain, I focused on his eyes, pushing into his mind. "Husband," was the message I pushed. Something pushed back. The spirit felt my invasion and the threat and fought harder. Lazlo's breathing shifted. He was in pain. He brought his head closer to mine; whether, by accident or a measure of him winning or nearly collapsing in pain, it was difficult to tell. The blasts in the background combined with Maeve and Ana's shouting were distracting, but Ana was holding her own and so far, not spinning.

I was afraid Lazlo was losing his battle. He didn't look good. I risked exposure, lifting my hand against the force that was draining it to grab his face and bring his eyes back to mine. "I love you, Laz, please come back to me." My breath was shallow, but I managed. What a crappy time to finally say those words, but I wasn't sure if I'd get another chance. "Besekdlsa, he needs you," I whispered, wondering if the dragon could offer aid.

I could see his fight escalating; it was all on his face. His expressions were contorted, shifting. Despite my best effort, it didn't look promising. He grabbed my hand and set it back on the arm, holding it down. Then out of the air, from seemingly nowhere, a talon appeared next to his head. It touched him; a blue light flooded him. His eyes flashed. He gripped my hand and placed it over the amulet, holding his hand over mine, then he kissed me. It was a suffocating kiss in my current state, but he quickly backed off as he channeled my energy and that of the amulet into himself. He was pushing the spirit out, sending it back behind the gate. My head was spinning from my pain, but I could tell as he breathed a deep sigh that his efforts were successful. He held my eyes again. This time our connection was back. "Mother is distracted, I need to get you out of this thing, but quickly so she doesn't have time to react." He silently unfastened my other hand, looking back to make sure Maeve was still occupied with Ana before he untied my neck and head, all of which he could do while blocking her view. The pain was getting worse. I was near to losing consciousness and could feel myself slipping. I saw Lazlo nod to me before quickly kneeling, and with brut force, he ripped both of the foot restraints off at the same time.

As Maeve heard the sound and turned to see what was happening, he scooped me into his arms, and all of the gemstones rolled away, the drain ceasing as he moved me further away from them. Before she could respond, he pulled me through a dark archway, and we were back inside the gate room.

"We don't have much time. She may abandon Ana to get to us." He lowered my legs while still holding me against him. I was weak but conscious. "Once more with the amulet. We are taking this thing down together."

He put my hand on the amulet, his on top of mine. We channeled our combined magic. I recited the spell from my book to aid the spirits in crossing. Lazlo worked with his magic to dismantle the cage that held them. I felt the gate itself falling bit by bit, pieces locking away. As I sensed the last one slam shut, we heard Maeve running around the corner.

"Lazlo, no!" But even if he had wanted to listen to her, it was too late. Almost instantly, we heard the rumble. It quickly became louder. "These walls are held with that magic, Lazlo. The manor is falling!" Maeve shouted over the roars starting to fill the building.

Ana was rushing up behind Maeve, sword in hand. Maeve

turned toward her, and in an instant, she was gone, simply vanished, and Ana's sword came crashing into the floor. We all looked around. It was clear we didn't have much time.

Ruins

"Head for the entrance Ana, we'll be right behind you" Lazlo shouted as he once again lifted me in his arms and started to run. I was relieved when we made it to the top of the stairs and could see the entryway of the manor, although chunks were falling all around us. Both Lazlo and Ana had to dodge as if they were running an obstacle course. I clutched Lazlo tighter, feeling useless and as if I were an extra burden. At last, we made it to the door and out onto the grounds in front of the estate. The horrifying hunters had vanished as well. Lazlo sat me down on the grass then joined me. There was nothing we could do but watch as his family home crumbled.

"That part isn't falling," I noted with some hope.

"That is the original part of the building. It might suffer some damage, but it will survive since it was built before my family began to draw from the ancestral magic. Thankfully, that is where our bedroom is, so we still have a place to sleep tonight." He looked up at Ana. "Ana, my friend." Lazlo called her back from the daze she seemed to be in, staring off into the distance. "It seems we need to talk about secrets you've been keeping. If I understood correctly, I have a half-sibling. Gwen and I would have both been here for you; you should have told us."

She sat down next to Lazlo. "I know. I'm sorry. I'm really sorry." Tears were forming in her eyes. It was strange to see.

"You don't believe what Mother said, do you? That he wasn't going to follow through with you? She wouldn't have turned him into a wolf if he hadn't said he was leaving her. She'd have brought him back and made his life miserable. Trust me, Ana, I know my parents. Are you going after him, now that you know?"

"Are you going to search for him?" She asked.

"Marjorie and I will work together to lay the groundwork and attempt to figure out where he might be. With our home now in ruins, we won't be able to leave right away. Still, it may need to sooner rather than later since we don't know what Mother may still have planned and I need to keep Marjorie safe. So where may I ask is my new relative?"

Ana smiled. "He's with your father's family. I left him with them when I went to serve the Goddess. They were happy to have him, especially since they thought Jordan was dead, like most of us. So yes, I'll appeal to my order for permission to hunt for him."

"Well, perhaps a trip to my father's family home will be our first stop."

He turned to me. "How are you feeling?"

"A bit better now that we are away from all of that." There had been so much information thrown at me, at all of us, it was difficult to sort out. But Lazlo seemed to be taking his father's apparent infidelity and appearance of a half brother in stride. For my part, I was still trying to sort through all Maeve had told me about my parents. Things were undoubtedly clearer now though.

We sat there for a while, watching things fall apart. Ana left to return to her order. I wondered what was being lost in this chaos, what family treasures were buried. I was thankful to know that our personal belongings, specifically all of the things I had left from my old life, were safe in the original part of the building.

I wondered what had happened to Maeve, what her next move was likely to be. In his true supportive fashion, Lazlo turned to me and smiled. No questions, no judgment. "Things will be alright" was all he said as we sat there and watched.

After what felt like hours, the chaos seemed to come to an end. A side entrance was clear of rubble, so we made our way inside. The kitchen was still intact, as was the narrow staircase that we followed up and found ourselves in the original wing of the manor. Both of us exhausted, we slid into bed. Lazlo held me in his arms, and I drifted quickly into a deep sleep.

Rude Awakening

I woke with a pounding headache; light from the window was burning my eyes. The world felt as if it was spinning. What had happened? I reached out next to me. This wasn't our bed. Lazlo wasn't there. I was in my apartment in New York City. An empty whiskey bottle was on the windowsill. Was I dreaming?

"Hey there, Margie. I wasn't sure how long you were going to sleep," Chris said.

Chris? Where did he come from? I distinctly remember turning down his offer the night before I left, yet here he was in my bedroom getting dressed. Was this some old memory?

"I think we both got a bit carried away with the whiskey last night. You were seriously putting them down. How're you feeling?"

"Like shit," I managed to say. My head was still spinning. How did I get here? Where was Lazlo?

"Well, I hate to fun and run, but I've got to get to work. Thanks for the book, by the way," he said, lifting a book from the table and heading out the door.

As I watched him walk away with that book in his hand, the signature hit me. I wanted to throw up. Somehow in a drunken frenzy that I had no recollection of, I had given an innocent a cursed book. There was no way to take that action back, that much I knew. That book wouldn't let me anywhere near it, not until Chris passed it on to yet another innocent.

Was everything I thought had happened merely a story in that book? I could see my bags still packed. That part was the same. Had I somehow been sent back to the past? I frantically searched my bags but could find no sign of Lazlo's letter. My heart felt like it would explode. Tears began to run down my face. I couldn't contain my sobbing. Could I really have lost him? Did I ever really have him? I still felt such a strong love for him, such a pull toward him. Was he even real?

After a good crying fit, I steeled myself. I had already told the landlady I was leaving. I had to honor that. I was homeless, a gypsy. I had no one and no place to go. I could already feel the book pushing me away. Perhaps I could find another mage who could help. The possibility wasn't strong, but I had to try.

I wandered out onto the street. Grand Central seemed the place to go even if I didn't have a mysterious letter or invitation. I felt so empty, but I knew I had to connect with someone. I couldn't just let Chris or someone near him die or be hurt. It was the only thought moving my feet forward, even if it was at a slow and reluctant pace.

Making my way from the subway to the station, I heard a saxophone echoing in the halls. This time the tune sounded darker. "Stormy Weather" was the song I recognized after a moment. I fought back the tears again. It wasn't fair. I felt things I'd never felt before, and it was all a dream, a story in a book. I wandered about the station, trying to find some connection with where I would go.

Suddenly, someone from the shadows signaled me.

"Over here, Miss," he beckoned.

Now, crossing to a stranger standing in a shadowed area of Grand Central Station in New York City admittedly isn't a wise thing. Still, at this point, I felt my life, as I thought I knew it, was over. What truly did I have to lose? My life? It was worthless as far as I was concerned right then. Maybe I could save Chris, or maybe not. What did it really matter? The voices in my head were persistent. "Go" is what I heard. "Go to him." So I took a few steps in his direction.

Bright green eyes shone from his face. His attire was that of a beggar, but his face was different; not entirely human, with a surreal sheen to his skin. I didn't see any need to pretend not to stare. A few strands of jet black hair hung across his face, loose from his knit cap. His hand, clad in a black fingerless glove, reached out for me.

"That's right. Come with me now," he said, his hand still extended and his eyes dancing in anticipation. "It's alright. Lost much, have you? I see the sadness in those eyes. Come, all will be well."

Every logical bone in my body said, run away, this is creepy, but I kept moving toward him despite the voice inside me working on getting through the ringing hangover screaming no. I reached my hand out to his, our fingers touched. I heard Lazlo's voice crying out my name. Darkness swirled around me as I attempted to turn in that direction. I thought I saw the outline of his tall, muscular form. My heart leapt. Was he real after all? Then it all disappeared; everything went black.

In the darkness, small lights began to appear, sparkling all around. The sensation was one of being pulled through a tunnel and then pushed down a slide; swirling fast motion. Just when I thought my mind would explode, it stopped. My feet were on the ground again. A large wooden door appeared.

There was no sign of the man I had seen in the station, only darkness, blinking lights, and the door, which was glowing on all edges as if the light was leaking from the next room.

As I stepped closer to the door and reached for the handle, it opened without my touch. Bright white light flooded everything and my eyes felt blinded by the intensity. The door closed behind me with a loud thud.

"Welcome, granddaughter," came a soft voice from nearby. "We have waited all these years to finally meet you. We rejoice that you are among us now."

The Missing Bride

A sharp pain ripped through Lazlo's chest, waking him from his sleep. His eyes opened wide, his heart racing, he surveyed the room. Marjorie wasn't next to him. Something was wrong. The things Marjorie had brought with her, the guitar, her bags, her book; they were gone. Where was she?

He jumped out of bed, dressing as he made his way down the remaining staircase in the manor.

"Marjorie!" he called, hoping she had simply woken and was exploring the area. The silence he heard in return was deafening. The pain in his chest was still present as if something was being pulled out of him. He sensed that somehow the magical bond that he and Marjorie shared was being challenged. Different magics were at work here; he could feel them. But where was she, and who was doing this?

It took every bit of strength he had not to fall back to the young man who had been devastated when Marjorie's grandmother had spirited her away, and she had been lost to his life for those twelve years. He'd worked hard to forget her, to move on. But as soon as she'd walked back in, she was all he'd wanted. This couldn't be happening again, not now that they were married. This wasn't her choice, he told himself; it couldn't be.

Lazlo quickly made his way to the stables and saddled a horse. The window to where he sensed Marjorie would be was small, so he had to hurry. The train had brought her here. If he hurried, it would take him there. He pushed the horse faster as they traveled down the road from the manor to the train station.

"I need to get to New York City," he informed the ticket attendant upon his arrival at the window.

"Well, in luck you are; the last train leaves in fifteen minutes. Traveling kind of light, aren't you? You do know the window won't open up from there again for another three weeks, don't you?"

"Thanks for that information. I'll make do, but I need to be on that train."

"Right then, M'Lord, we'll get your animal safely back. I'll notify your man, Arthur. Good luck."

Lazlo jumped onto the train and slid into a seat. He breathed a sigh of relief that at least he'd made it this far.

"Say aren't you Queen Maeve's boy? Lazlo, right? Or Lord DuLaene now, aren't you?" a tall, slender man with slicked-back brown hair in a brown suit asked him.

"Do I know you?" he inquired. "Or do you know my mother?"

"Neither dear boy, I merely am a man with my ear to the ground, I hear things, I notice things, I seek opportunities. For instance, I heard you recently wed, yet I notice she isn't here with you now? Lost your bride already?"

"Truly, you are a gifted individual. Not only do you notice things, but you seem to have an uncanny ability to make someone dislike you within seconds of meeting you." Lazlo replied.

The man slid into the seat across from Lazlo as the train began to pull out of the station. "Ah now, no need to get disgruntled. No judgment; I was only making an observation." The man looked around Lazlo, his eyes scanning the area. "I also noticed that you seem to be missing any luggage. You're traveling to a foreign realm where you'll be in a strange city for up to three weeks. Unless you have an alternate way out?" he inquired.

Lazlo shrugged. So far, this conversation was useless as far as he was concerned. He saw no need to say anything.

"I'm guessing it's your first time out there and that your missing bride is part of the reason. George Greenly is the name, by the way, and I'd be willing to help. Here's my card; you'll figure out how to reach me." He handed a small card to Lazlo, who looked at it curiously. Perhaps this man wasn't entirely useless.

"If you know anything, who has her, what I'm up against. That's the information I seek." Lazlo said.

"I may hear a thing or two. I heard Finnvara, the fae king, was looking for her. Your mother, of course, has an interest, but if you suspected her, you wouldn't be here, so something is pulling you differently. My guess is Fin. You see, Lord DuLaene, I sit in all the courts, in this land and others, I have eyes everywhere, and as an individual, with valuable information, I do require payment. What I've told you already is what I know and am willing to share. If you want to work with me, allow me to work with you, then more needs to be on the table, and don't bother threatening me; I've faced far more menacing individuals than you." George relaxed back into his seat with a smile.

Lazlo studied him. George was confident, extremely confident, and there must be a reason, and it didn't speak well of his character, of that Lazlo was sure.

"Well, George, nothing you've said gives me a desire to be in your circle. I'm confident in my abilities to find my wife and rescue her from anyone she may encounter."

George shrugged. "Suit yourself. Reach out if you change your mind."

The train went dark, and when the light returned, Lazlo was alone again. He looked around but saw no sign of George. When the train came to a stop, he bolted out and was surprised by this strange new place. His senses felt assaulted by the air. So many unusual smells; the ground was different. These structures were unlike anything he'd ever seen. Marjorie had talked about this place, but he never imagined it quite like this. He followed the crowd in hopes this would lead to the way out. Exactly how he would find her, he wasn't sure other than depending on the bond that they shared. He could feel it pulling him to her.

He walked briskly through the crowd, searching for her face, her shape. Ahead he could hear music, a rich, full sound unlike any he'd ever heard echoing through the enormous space. He saw her familiar shape, her jet black hair, and ran faster, calling out her name. He saw her stop and turn to him just before she disappeared into thin air. She was gone again. The tug was still there, the bond intact, but now he was completely unsure of the direction he should follow.

He looked around; this place was far more alien than he had expected. He pulled out the card that George had handed him and wondered what his options were.

About the Author

Vee R. Paxton is a Portland, Oregon-based author with a love of writing fantasy, romance, and the occasional erotica.

You can connect with me on:
- https://www.facebook.com/fantasyromanceauthor
- https://www.instagram.com/veerpaxton

Made in the USA
Columbia, SC
13 July 2021